DEFENDERS
—OF THE—
VALLEY

Pat Coleman

Scripture Union
130 City Road, London EC1V 2NJ

By the same author:
Race the Wind (Tiger Book)
Smugglers' Cove (Tiger Book)
Midnight Traveller (Leopard Book)
© Pat Coleman 1989
First published 1989

ISBN 0 86201 562 6

Phototypeset by Input Typesetting Ltd, London
Printed and bound in Great Britain by Cox and Wyman Ltd, Reading

Chapter One

'The weather was good, and the sheep didn't have to come in early and dry off before the wool clip.' Peter James decided that his listening friend looked confused, and he added kindly, 'Wool clip means shearing, giving the sheep a hair cut. The shearing gang was really quick – zip, zip with the electric clippers, and one bald sheep!'

Peter had talked non-stop since he left the house, his blue eyes bright with excitement and his thin shoulders squared with pride. Now he pulled his peaked cap down over his fair, almost white hair, and looked embarrassed.

He said, 'Too much talk about the farm, Seb?'

Seb Craig grinned. 'No problem.' He was twelve which made him one year older than his friend.

Peter propped his elbows on the drystone garden wall and gazed at the green valley and, beyond it, the high hills called fells in this part of the country. Sheep grazed on the hills, and on the hot sunny day they looked like smudges of snow on the grassy slopes.

'When I first came, I wondered if the sheep had special short legs on one side so they could keep their balance. The fields are so steep, you see.'

'And do they?' asked Seb who didn't know, but was always eager to learn.

'No, Cheviots are hill sheep and sure-footed – most of the time anyway, but they can fall in holes and things, and then you have to get them out.'

Seb Craig settled his glasses on his short nose and nodded wisely. He admired sure-footedness in people and animals, too, but he knew all about stumbling. Sometimes his feet seemed to have a life of their own. His mother said that he was improving as he grew, but Seb couldn't see it. He still was among the last to be chosen for school sports teams.

Peter said, 'I really like it here at the farm. It's great. Uncle's teaching me all about raising sheep, and I'm going to be a farmer when I grow up, just like I always wanted. Remember how I talked about it last summer?'

They both went silent, recalling the events of the previous summer when Seb Craig, his cousin Fiona and their new friend, Mike, had saved Peter James from his rotten stepfather and sent him to his Aunt Dora.* God had helped, too, Peter thought. Why else had Seb and Fiona shown up when things were really bad and he was sniffing glue? They had liked him straight away and joined forces with Mike to help him. God had sent him the best of friends when he needed them most. It made him feel good just to think about it.

The boys turned at the sound of a door slamming. Fiona came flying around the side of the house and down the garden path, her ginger plaits streaming in her own breeze. As usual her socks were wrinkled down around her ankles and her shirt was adrift from her jeans. Fiona was ten years old, and the boys agreed privately that she was bossy but that she made up for it with her sharp wits and kindness.

She slid to a stop beside them and her brown eyes were serious. 'Your aunt's upset and your uncle looks like thunder. I think the morning post did it. I heard your uncle say, "The world's gone mad! Prime grazing land given over to tennis courts and chalets! I'm going

* This story is told in *Smugglers' Cove*

6

up the wall." Your aunt poured him a coffee, and he drank half before he settled down again.'

Peter frowned. Uncle upset? It must be serious. Uncle was the most even-tempered of men. And good grazing land given over to chalets? What was going on?

Seb said, 'Fiona, you're not supposed to eavesdrop.'

'How else could I find out what was going on?' she responded reasonably, as if it were the only logical thing to do. 'Besides I had every right to be there. I thought there might be a letter from Mike.'

'Why should Mike write when he'll be here soon?'

'Well, I wrote to him last night, a long letter all about the two of us coming up here together on the train from London yesterday, and how we didn't get lost – '

'Why should we get lost? We didn't change trains and Peter met us at the station!'

'- and how everybody's been terrific and how nice the farm is,' Fiona finished calmly as if there had been no interruption. 'Anyway, what's it all about?'

Peter swallowed hard. 'Dunno.'

'Then I'd better tell you what else I happened to hear when I was outside the kitchen. It seems a development company wants to buy Viking Farm to build a tourist complex. Your uncle said he'd sooner cross the Sahara Desert on his hands and knees than sell.'

'Good for him,' Peter said in a not quite steady voice.

He stared at the house, seeing the white painted walls thick and strong to keep out the sometimes fierce weather, the grey slate roof and the colourful flowers in the front garden. The barn and outbuildings were behind the farmhouse, laid out around a cobblestone yard. He could see the sheep pens and dipping trough if he leaned to one side. The hills might be bare, but here in the valley – his aunt called it a dale – trees were all over the place, old, tall and kind of friendly to a boy who had found a wonderful new home and family.

All of it was perfect and he loved it. If the farm were ever sold, if he couldn't live in this perfect place, he would – Peter searched his mind for his own reaction – he would die!

Seb spoke up. 'Peter, stop looking like a ghost. Your uncle won't sell, that's clear enough. Fiona might be nosey, but you can bet she heard right.' He polished his glasses on his T-shirt.

Fiona backed him. 'If you don't cheer up, Peter, I'll be sorry I ever mentioned it. You look like you did last summer, scared, and there's no reason.'

Peter pulled himself together. In the year he had lived with Uncle John, Aunt Dora and his two older cousins he had come a long way from the frightened, confused boy he had been. He had found love and understanding in full measure, and panicking at the first hint of trouble made a nonsense of his hard-won confidence.

'You're right. Uncle John's the finest man I ever knew, and if he says he won't sell, he won't. Let's forget it.'

Seb nodded, satisfied that his mate was back on form. 'What'll we do today? I vote for starting in the village, suss out the ice cream supply, so to speak.'

'Right,' said Peter.

Fiona said, 'I'll get my postcard list. I promised all my friends cards.'

Seb sighed. 'You always promise your friends postcards. You spend half your holidays writing.'

'Pooh! You complained like mad when I didn't send you one at Easter!'

'That's different. I'm your cousin.'

Peter stepped in. 'Give over, you two, or we'll never get started.'

The narrow lane to the village was an ancient way, rising in a long curve from Viking Farm and by-passing a height which overlooked the valley. The lane was shaded by old trees with thick trunks and soaring branches that touched overhead. Nearing the village the slope steepened and grey stone cottages appeared, tucked into the base of the height.

Seb and Fiona's eyes were everywhere, following the flight of a bird or inspecting the quiet cottages. Once a Landrover passed, hauling a trailer loaded with farm machinery. Later a car with a family of tourists drove by, and the children in the back seat pulled faces at them until they rounded the bend and were out of sight.

Peter led the way, keeping to the worn verge beside the tarmac lane, pointing out the things of interest. 'That's where I get the school bus, up ahead at the T-junction where the shelter is, and that's a shop and post office, there where the post box is.'

When he thought about it, there didn't seem to be much to show them, but Seb and Fiona were agreeably wide-eyed.

Abruptly Seb said, 'That's funny.'

Peter turned around to see him looking up at the tree-covered height, shading his eyes against the sun.

Seb shrugged and continued walking. 'I thought I saw something up at the top, but I couldn't have.'

'What couldn't you have seen?' asked Fiona.

'Well, I was looking up there – ' he pointed to the top of the height, ' – and I saw some grey stone, like the battlements of a castle tower, where the soldiers used to keep watch. But I can't have, because now I don't see anything but tree tops.'

Fiona shaded her eyes and looked in the direction of his pointing finger. 'I don't see anything.'

Peter walked back a few steps in the direction from which they had come. 'Try looking from here.'

They joined him and again looked up. Peter said, 'This is the only spot on the lane where you can see Acre Castle. The trees hide it, and you wouldn't know it was there unless you knew where to look. See? Up there, where those two treetops don't meet? That's where you'll see the battlements.'

Fiona moved slightly sideways and squealed in pleasure. 'I see it now. A castle, a proper castle. Fabulous!'

Peter swelled with pride, for all the world as if he owned it. 'It's not very big,' he said modestly, 'but it's been there since the Crusades. A knight came back here and built it, named it after Acre, the sea port where the Crusaders fought.'

'Let's go and see it!' said Fiona and Seb in unison.

'Sorry, but it's not open to the public. It's privately owned, and somebody lives there, but we can see it from the gate if you like.'

'Better than nothing,' Seb assured him. 'Lead on.'

They walked on until they came to a track the width of a car. A few houses with small front gardens stood at one side and on the other a high stone wall with lichen and small ferns growing from the cracks.

Peter said, 'The gate's up there at the end of the track.'

Once they passed the houses it seemed even quieter. The track curved on and up, and their footsteps hardly sounded on the hard-packed earth. At their side the shadows were deep and black in the woods. The air was still in the enclosed space, and Seb wiped his moist forehead with the back of his hand. When a bird unexpectedly flew out from the trees, cawing loudly, they jumped and exchanged embarrassed glances.

Fiona said softly, 'Sort of lonely. I don't think I'd like to live here.'

Seb cleared his throat. 'Who owns the castle?'

'Miss Haverly. I saw her in church once,' said Peter, keeping his voice low as the others had done. 'She's old as the hills and keeps to herself. Has her groceries delivered to the gate and doesn't collect them until the driver's gone. I don't think she likes people much. Here we are.'

The track finished and as one they slowed at the sight of rusting wrought-iron gates sagging on their hinges. The stone gateposts were topped by grotesque figures of lions that reared and pawed the air and seemed to snarl at them in the shaded light of the thick trees.

They advanced slowly and peered carefully around the nearer of the two worn gateposts. Cloud passed over the sun, and the light grew suddenly dim in this isolated spot. Peter gave a small shiver.

Fiona whispered, 'Are you sure it's okay to look?'

Peter nodded silently, but he couldn't help feeling hesitant all the same. He had come to look at Acre Castle only once before, and now he remembered why he had never returned. The place was spooky.

Beyond the gates a weed-strewn gravel drive led to a grey stone building, built square on the high point of land. There were four levels. The ground level had no windows at all, but the upper three were marked by darkened windows ranging from arrow slits to the large casement sort with leaded panes, hinged to open at the side.

At the very top, as they had seen from the lane, was a crenellated wall with a saw-tooth pattern and a small tower at each of the four corners. From here, in a long ago age, a sentry would have kept a check on the valley and the roads below. An arched wooden door with iron studs was the only entrance in sight.

'Strictly speaking, it's a keep, not a castle,' Seb said, scratching at his sun-burned cheek in thought. 'A keep was part of a castle, the central tower. Maybe the knight ran out of money before he could build the rest.'

'Who cares?' said Fiona. 'I think it's beautiful! Brilliant! Aren't you lucky, Peter, having your very own castle right on your doorstep? How I wish we could see inside.'

'And, I daresay, have a cup of tea!' came a sharp, thin voice from nowhere.

The children gasped. Fiona grabbed Peter's arm and hung on for dear life. Seb stepped back onto Peter's foot, and Peter grunted loudly. As one they inched back along the track.

A small figure suddenly appeared at the gates and glared at them through the bars. She was thin and wiry with a nut brown face, seamed and lined by the weather. Wisps of grey hair stuck out wildly in all directions from beneath her broad brimmed straw hat, and in one hand she held a wicker basket filled with weeds.

Peter found his voice first. 'We didn't think any such thing, Miss Haverly.' Seb and Fiona shook their heads madly in agreement. 'We were just passing, and we stopped to look through the gate.' He hoped that God would not notice his lie, but he felt desperate. His plans never included meeting the owner of Acre Castle.

'Just passing,' Seb muttered loyally.

By now they had backed a few feet from the entrance. Fiona's fingers were digging into Peter's arm.

'Just passing, lad? Some story! It's a good long walk up from the lane, and nothing beyond here. What do you say to that, eh!' the woman barked, thrusting her head forward until Peter feared she would be caught between the bars. She had a front tooth missing. Given a big hooked nose, she would look like a witch in the fairy tales he once read.

He longed to turn and run, but he kept talking. 'We didn't mean anything, honest. I'm sorry if we disturbed you. My friends saw your house from the lane, and well, they like castles and – '

'Your friend was right, lad, this is a keep, not a castle.'

Fiona was pulling frantically at his arm, but he could not turn away from the sharp black eyes that seemed to bore into him. From behind him the sound of Seb's rapid breathing was loud.

Peter said, 'Seb's usually right. He's got more'n his

fair share of brains. We'll be going now. Thank you for – ' His voice faltered. Thank you for what? Miss Haverly hadn't done anything except bark at them and scare them half to death. All the same Aunt Dora would expect him to mind his manners, even if he wished he'd never come.

'Thank you for everything,' he finished in a rush. Now for a lightning sprint back down the track and out of sight of this weird place.

Miss Haverly's eyes narrowed. 'I know you from somewhere.'

'My uncle owns Viking Farm. I saw you once in church.'

Miss Haverly suddenly smiled. The gap in her front teeth looked like the Channel Tunnel. 'I remember. You helped me.'

He turned and prepared to run as fast as his legs could carry him, when the woman demanded, 'Just a minute. Where do you think you're going?'

Chapter Two

Miss Haverly drew an iron key from her pocket and unlocked the gate. 'Sharp young eyes for searching, that's what I need,' she said. 'I've lost my favourite scissors, little ones for snipping threads. You three – ' Peter, Seb and Fiona listened wide-eyed in astonishment. 'You three'll find them in a flash.'

The wrought-iron gates were open. She gestured impatiently. 'Don't stand there like moonlings, come in, come in.'

Peter hesitated. Fiona had been eager to see inside, but the alarm on her face said clearly that she had changed her mind. He couldn't blame her. Miss Haverly was really peculiar.

Seb stepped forward. 'And could we look around inside the castle, Miss Haverly? I've never seen one that was lived in, and I'm interested.'

'Yes, yes, but hurry along. I need my scissors.'

Seb shot through the open gate and fell in step with the owner, pointing eagerly to the stone building and asking questions.

Fiona groaned. 'That Seb! We should've known he couldn't resist a chance to learn something new.'

'You're telling me! Come on, we'd better go with him.'

They trudged up the overgrown gravel driveway in silence toward the iron-studded wooden door set into the wall, a door deliberately built narrow so that only one person could pass through at a time. Miss Haverly called, 'That door's rusted shut. The entrance is this way.'

They rounded the corner and came to a tall flight of steps which ran up the side of the wall and led to a door on the first floor. Seb told his friends, 'When the keep was operational, the steps were a form of defence against attack.'

'Great!' muttered Fiona. 'He's off again. I'll bet we get the whole history of Norman castle building before he's finished.'

Seb went on, 'Attackers had to climb the steps to get to the door, and on the little landing they couldn't build up a good swing when they used something like a battering ram to break it down. And only a few could stand there at one time, and all the time boiling oil and rocks would be dropping, and arrows would be whistling around 'em,' he finished with relish.

Peter cared little about castles, if the truth were told. His heart was with the farm and the animals and the cycle of work which followed the seasons. But Seb's enthusiasm was infectious, and Peter began to wonder about the knight who had lived there. A veteran of the battle of Acre, a seaport of Israel, in the third Crusade, his teacher had said. The knight had returned home, received a 'licence to crenellate' from the king, and built his stronghold. Just like planning permission today, Peter's teacher had explained.

The main door of Acre Castle opened onto a stone lobby with a wooden floor. A richly patterned carpet lay on the floor. A table with a bowl of fresh roses and a telephone stood against a wall. What had he expected to see? The knight himself in full armour?

Miss Haverly set a brisk pace. The adjoining room was almost in darkness with heavy curtains drawn across the windows. Peter peered about, glimpsing a fireplace and furniture before they were hurried through to the dining room. In here Peter only had time to see that the room was large, dim and dusty before they were in the kitchen.

The kitchen was another matter. It was very nearly cheerful, compared to the rooms they had dashed through. The morning sunshine poured through tall, arched windows. A handsome marmalade cat with a green collar lay curled up on the cushion of a rocking chair and woke up long enough to lick one orange and white paw before settling back to sleep. A huge coal-fired range stood inside what had been a fireplace and would keep the room warm in winter as well as cook food. In one corner beside a bookshelf was a comfortable easy chair, well cushioned.

Miss Haverly hurried to the Welsh dresser and poked anxiously among the dishes on the open shelves. 'Maybe I put them down here–' She looked around sharply. 'Now, children, you've seen the castle, start looking for my scissors.'

Seen the castle? Peter and Seb exchanged indignant looks.

Fiona took charge. 'Seb, you search the room from the range to the scullery. Peter, start at the range and work past the windows. I'll do the rest.' She joined Miss Haverly at the dresser and opened the first drawer.

Peter crouched and looked under the range. Some crumbs, dust and a spider that looked back at him. No scissors. Peter decided against opening the oven door. In his wildest imagination he could not imagine scissors being found in an oven.

Miss Haverly kept up a running commentary. 'I've misplaced so many things recently. My silver-backed hairbrush – how can I do my hair properly without it? – my photograph album – it's always in the bookshelf – my beautiful sunhat –'

At this Fiona looked up. 'Sunhat?'

'With red poppies on the brim. Goodness, girl, don't look so surprised!' She touched the battered sunhat which she had not bothered to remove. 'Do you think I'd wear this thing if I didn't have to?'

Fiona turned away to hide a smile. 'No, Miss Haverly.'

Fiona found the scissors. Naturally, thought Peter. She was the efficient one and probably the only one among them who would think to lift the seat cushion from the easy chair.

'Splendid, just splendid,' declared the pleased owner as she tucked them into her sewing basket. 'Now we shall have tea. I never drink coffee in the mornings, don't keep the nasty stuff in the house.'

Peter slid his chair next to Seb's and sat down at the table. He needed the solid comfort of his mate's nearness. The morning was turning into a crazy fantasy of dark corners and cold stone walls.

When Miss Haverly placed a silver tray on the table, set with delicately thin china and a silver tea pot, Peter's face went stiff at the sight. He could see exactly what was going to happen, could picture it in his mind as if it had already happened. He would take the elegant cup and saucer from Miss Haverly, and they would drop from his rough, clumsy hands that were more used to handling sheep and farm tools than fancy china.

Or if it didn't happen then, the cup would drop when he picked it up to drink. At either time the china would certainly finish on the kitchen floor, smashed to pieces. It would have to be replaced, and he would be without pocket money for years. He squirmed in agony.

'Help yourselves to fruitcake,' Miss Haverly said. 'It's my own baking. Anne and Mary forgot to give me a cake for my birthday.'

Peter came to his cousins' defence. 'They're away. Anne's working in town this summer and Mary's looking for digs at college. If they'd been here, they'd have remembered.'

He could no longer ignore the tea which Miss Haverly had placed before him. The cup sat there like an alien monster, waiting to destroy him, and he eyed it fearfully. Ask and you shall receive, Jesus had taught. Very well. Please, Jesus, send me steady hands, he pleaded desperately.

He took a deep breath and carefully placed both hands on the now cooler cup, raised it to his lips and drank without pausing. He replaced the empty cup in the saucer, just as carefully let go and put his hands in his lap. It was done. The worst had not happened, and he was safe. Thank you, Jesus, he said silently. I owe you one.

A few minutes later the children said their goodbyes and left. Out of sight on the track they stopped and looked at each other.

Seb said, 'That was something!'

'You bet!' Fiona sniffed the good, clean air gratefully. 'Imagine Miss Haverly interested in hats! Her clothes were dreadful, so old fashioned.'

Seb's face twisted in thought. 'Why did she remember you from church, Peter?'

He laughed out loud. 'She dropped the collection plate, and the money went everywhere. I helped her pick it up.'

'Did she really?' demanded Fiona, fascinated. 'I always dread it happening when the plate comes to me. Ours is wood, so it's very heavy.'

Seb said, 'I'd have liked to see the castle stairways set in the walls. And the cellar – that was the ground floor without windows. We didn't see much of anything.'

'You noticed,' Fiona said dryly. 'As Mike would say, we were had. The tea things were pretty, weren't they, Peter?'

'Mmm. Let's get on to the shop.' Not for the world

would Peter admit to what he had suffered at the table.

The rest of the day passed so quickly that Peter was surprised when bedtime came. He shared his room with Seb – a third bed would be brought in for Mike – and when he returned from his bath, Seb was already saying his prayers. Peter kneeled beside his bed and prepared to do the same. There was a lot to talk to God about.

He began with more thanks for the visit of his friends and went on to say, 'We had a peculiar morning at Acre Castle. That Miss Haverly is weird. She brought out her best china for us! I was scared I'd break it, but I had a quick word with Jesus, and he saw me through okay. This afternoon Fiona, Seb and I wandered all over the farm, and Uncle John let me take Barney and practise herding the sheep. That's one smart dog! Fiona and Seb laughed like anything when I tried to move some Cheviots from one field to the next – I'm not very good at it yet – but Barney knew what I wanted. In the end he moved them nearly on his own.'

Peter waited. Something else niggled, something more he wanted to say. It came. 'Somebody wants to buy Viking Farm, but Uncle John won't sell, and I'm glad. You know that I love my family and the farm, so please let me stay here for ever and ever. Amen.'

Seb was already in bed. Peter scrambled into his and turned off the light. 'Goodnight, Seb.'

The door flew open. Fiona stood there in her dressing gown. 'I've been waiting ages for somebody to come and say goodnight!'

'Goodnight, Fiona,' they sang out.

'That's better. Goodnight to you.' She closed the door and they fell promptly asleep.

Viking Farm's only cow was named Daisy. She had black and white patches and stood at the field gate, looking mournful, when the three children arrived to milk her next morning. Seb carried two clean pails, Fiona carried a milking stool, and Peter looked important. He would do the actual milking and in the field itself this morning. Daisy didn't care if she were milked here or in the barn. She was a friendly cow.

The air was warming up, the sun shone gently in the early morning sky and sent long shadows across the field. Rabbits fed on the grass near the safety of the trees. Peter enjoyed the awed look that Seb gave him as he worked the streams of Daisy's rich warm milk into the pail. Seb's admiration was to be treasured. Peter knew that he wasn't as clever as his friend, and he was grateful that he could do something that his friend couldn't.

They fed the chickens that provided eggs for the farm, Barney the sheepdog and then Missy, the other sheepdog who had recently produced a fine litter of future working dogs. Fiona was soppy over the squirming bundles of fur, but Peter and Seb kept their hands in their pockets and looked on in a superior way that showed they were above Fiona's cooing and aahing over the pups.

After breakfast they walked to the shop for Aunt Dora.

Fiona said, 'The stamps for my cards'll cost a fortune.'

'Don't write so many,' was Seb's unsympathetic reply.

Peter stopped. 'Listen.' From the distance came the unmistakable sound of a motorcycle.

'A motorbike,' said Fiona, eyeing him curiously. 'So what's new?'

'That'll be Leonard. He's a real tearaway. All he does is race along the roads and make trouble. Let's walk farther away from the road. He likes to show off and scare kids.'

'D'you know him?' Seb asked.

'He helps Uncle John around the farm sometimes. Just keep walking and don't pay him any attention.'

The sound of the motorbike drew close. Peter's mouth tightened. What would he do if Leonard stopped? Wait and see what Leonard would do next. And if he went for them with his bike? Dodge. But what about Seb and Fiona? Fiona was like quicksilver, but Seb might fall over his own feet, right in the path of the motorbike!

It was beside them now, the engine sounding big and powerful and exploding the peace of the morning. Peter kept walking. The roar lessened. Leonard was slowing up.

'Hey, Peter, how's tricks?' came the familiar voice.

He looked sideways. Leonard all right. Black leather jacket and all the gear of the motorcyclist. He steered the slowly moving machine, keeping pace with them. Beneath his crash helmet his sharp features were split in a knowing grin.

Peter said, 'Okay.'

'Who're your pals?'

'They're visiting me from London.'

'Big city kids, eh?'

'That's right.'

Leonard sneered. 'I don't like big city kids. Know-it-alls.'

'My friends aren't like that.' Peter scowled.

'No, we aren't,' exclaimed Seb, stung by such injustice, and came to a stop. Peter bumped into him. Fiona looked around and stopped, too.

'Not talking to you, four eyes.' Leonard braked and put a booted foot onto the road to support the bike. He removed his helmet and ran a hand through his long dark hair. His gold earstud glinted in the sun. 'Like I said, all city kids are wet, no guts. Spraying walls with aerosols, that's all they're good for.'

'We don't! And don't talk to my cousin like that!' Fiona practically danced in rage. Leonard looked her over and laughed. Fiona's brown eyes narrowed against her rising temper.

'Gonna give you a lot a treat. Gonna show you how a

pro handles a bike.'

Fiona was scornful. 'Pooh, you can't be a pro at your age.'

'Better believe it. I just turned seventeen, passed my test first go, and nobody, but nobody, rides like I do. Watch this.'

Leonard replaced his helmet, revved up his engine and sped off. For one hopeful moment Peter thought Leonard had gone for good, but seconds later he executed a neat tight u-turn and raced back on full throttle. The noise was deafening. Peter could scarcely think.

Leonard manoeuvred his machine in a fast series of sweeping curves that had him almost horizontal to the lane. He flashed by and returned, this time riding on his back wheel alone, the front wheel up in the air.

On the third pass he shouted, 'Watch my control.'

The words sent alarm signals through Peter's mind, and he instinctively moved back. 'Fiona, Seb, head for the trees! He'll try and clip our heels!'

The thought of the powerful, speeding machine coming within inches gave them extra speed as they raced for the protection of the trees. Peter's heart pounded. He heard the thunderous harsh sound of the motorbike following, coming closer and still closer. The trees, which before had seemed so near, now seemed to have shifted a mile away.

Peter was furious. Leonard was a ratfink. He thought he was tops but one slight misjudgement, and somebody could finish in hospital. Did Leonard ever think about that? No, he just swanned along, showing off, scaring everybody he could.

The trees were at hand. Peter jumped the remaining distance and whirled around, hand outstretched. Fiona bounded into the shelter beside him. Together they reached for Seb and jerked him the final distance to safety. The motorcycle flashed by, missing the tree by a hair's breadth, then spun away to the road.

Leonard raised his gloved fist in a gesture of triumph as he tore away.

Fiona tossed her ginger plaits back over her shoulders. 'He should be locked up. How does a scruff like that afford a motorbike anyway?' She was panting hard and her face was white with scarlet patches.

'Odd jobs. He helps Uncle John at lambing and shearing times.' Peter wished that his knees would stop wobbling. 'Uncle says he's good with animals, but I never did like him.'

'And now I don't either,' said Seb unsteadily.

Fiona took a deep breath and lifted her chin. 'Let's get on to the shop. I could use an ice cream.'

Chapter Three

Peter, Seb and Fiona could not forget the ugly incident with Leonard and his motorbike. They did Aunt Dora's shopping, bought stamps and posted Fiona's cards, ate ice creams, and still the fright and anger was there to be talked about.

Seb said on the way home, 'Something bad happens, and you can't forget it for ages.'

Peter screwed up his face. 'If only Mike'd been there, he'd have handled Leonard, maybe even sent him packing! Mike can handle anything.'

Fiona rounded on him. 'You handled it just fine, Peter James! Nobody got hurt and that's because you did the right things. Mike'd be the first to say so.'

Peter managed a grin, but he was not altogether convinced. Mike Bennett had that rare quality of leadership that Peter knew he himself would never have. Mike could lead a bunch of kids without even trying. Without even noticing, come to that. He'd probably finish up being Prime Minister.

Peter said, 'I miss Mike. I'll be glad to see him again.'

'Me, too, but he'll be here tomorrow,' Seb pointed out.

'What are we going to do about Leonard?' said Fiona, her mind busy with the problem at hand. 'How about carving him up and feeding him to the crows?'

'Fiona!' exclaimed Seb, shocked by the vehemence of

his normally kind relation.

She twisted the end of one ginger plait in embarrassment. 'I didn't really mean it. It just slipped out, but I feel quite sick, thinking of what Leonard did to us and all the terrible things I'd like to do to Leonard. D'you think that's why Jesus said to love your enemies and do good to them? That hating them only makes you feel worse?'

'Could be. But my Sunday School teacher says you also have to be on the guard against wickedness. And fight it, come to that. Very tricky at times, knowing the right thing to do.' Seb scratched his bony shoulder.

'Last summer we knew exactly what we had to do. We had to get Peter away from his rotten stepfather.'

'Right on! That was clear as anything.'

'But we probably haven't seen the last of Leonard.'

'We'll face that when the time comes,' Peter put in. 'But now, let's plan what we'll do this afternoon. Uncle said to check on the sheep in the east field today. How about it?'

The east field was wide and long. It began at the lane and extended to the top of the hill, separated from its neighbouring fields by drystone walls that ran upward to a point where the grazing became poor and neither sheep nor man bothered to venture. The walls might look rough and ready, but raising them was a skill. They were made of stone and rock, built up in layers so cleverly that no mortar was needed to hold them in place.

The three friends went to the field after lunch, the border collie Barney briskly trotting at their heels. Sheep were all over the place, eating their heads off.

Fiona scanned the field with some dismay. 'It's straight up!'

'Hardly!' protested Seb. 'Anyway, you don't have to come. You can always wait at the house.'

Peter grinned. They would hear no more complaints

from Fiona. She hated being left out of anything. He said, 'There are some rough spots – holes and a ledge. Uncle lost a sheep last winter when it slipped off the ledge in a storm, landed in a snowdrift and couldn't get out.'

'Poor thing,' said Fiona.

Seb sniffed. 'You're really daft. You moon over a sheep, but nobody likes lamb chops better'n you!'

'I expect it's because I don't really think of lamb chops as once being dear little woolly sheep.'

Peter opened the field gate, and they passed through.

Seb on a walking trip was a far cry from Seb on the playing fields. He knew about hiking from holidays on the coast, knew the dangers and satisfactions of walking in natural terrain. He had learned well the lessons of caution and preparation and moved with sharp aware-ness. On a hike he was as sure-footed as any mountain goat.

Peter led the way, having spent the past year acquaint-ing himself with the land. He walked tall with squared shoulders. Uncle had given him an important job, and he would do it the very best way he could.

For some distance the field was flat and even. This part was well grazed, the grass short and thick, and the walking was easy. The trained dog stayed near, following an interesting scent from time to time but never for long and returning promptly when called.

Fiona watched him admiringly. 'Not like some pets.'

'Barney's a working dog. He's not allowed in the house.' Then before Fiona could go all soppy over the poor lot of a working dog, Peter added hastily, 'It'd only confuse Barney. He's all business.' And then to Fiona's confusion, Peter reached down and affectionately ruffled Barney's black and white fur, exactly as if he were a real pet.

The small, hardy ewes and their lambs grazed quietly,

moving only to reach fresh grass. They lifted their heads as Peter approached to examine their condition with a critical eye. They looked fine. No limping or poorly look that could mean disease to be treated by the vet. No wounds that needed attention.

The afternoon passed as they criss-crossed the field to check each animal, walking ever higher as they progressed. Mid-way up the slope Peter showed them a fenced area in a jumble of rocks. Inside the paling fence was an open pit.

Peter said, 'Not very deep, but tricky all the same, and too tricky for sheep. Once in, they'd have to be pulled out. That's why Uncle fenced it.'

They had their tea on a flat rock overlooking the valley. From where they sat the tree-covered height and Acre Castle lay directly opposite.

Seb said, studying the mount, 'The castle's disappeared again behind the trees. If I didn't know it was there . . .'

Fiona asked, 'What're you doing, Peter? Don't tell me. You're counting sheep! So what do you count to get to sleep? Never mind, Seb and I'll count, too.'

Minutes later Peter put down his sandwich in sudden concern. 'One's missing. We all came up with the same tally, and it's not right. There should be one more.'

Fiona looked puzzled. 'How can one be missing? Where would it go?'

Peter's stomach moved uneasily. 'Down a hole maybe. Let's count again.'

They came up with the same figure a second time, and Peter gnawed his lip worriedly. 'What's worse, the one that's missing is the ewe Uncle entered at the local show. She won a prize.'

'How can you tell one from the other?'

'Uncle made a collar for her.'

Seb whistled softly, 'We'd better have a look at those

holes. How many?'

Peter pushed back his peaked cap and wiped his forehead with his forearm. 'Two. We already saw one of 'em.'

Fiona re-packed the uneaten sandwiches. 'Let's get started on the other one.'

Peter felt terrible, worried and half sick. This ewe was a beaut, tough with a strong mothering instinct. Any loss among the flocks was serious, but this would be a real tragedy.

Farther up the slope lay a broken tumble of rocks and tall grass surrounded by another fence of palings, and here the hole was a bad one. It took the form of a long, steep slope that continued down into the earth, practically for ever. Peter thought the hole looked like a big mouth, open and ready to swallow unsuspecting sheep – and boys – down its black, unseen throat.

If the sheep had forced a passage through the fence to get at the tempting grass and then gone down that angled slide . . . If it had broken bones . . . If it were dead . . .

A lamb stood nearby, looking lost and bleating loudly. Barney began to bark and circle restlessly. 'Heel, Barney!' Peter commanded. 'Listen.' The dog grew quiet and the bleating of another distressed sheep reached them, not loud and clear like the lamb's, but softly, as if it came from a great distance. A finger of fear brushed Peter's spine.

Fiona said in a small voice. 'Sounds like we've found it, and it's down there. What now?'

Seb said, 'Look! The fence has been pushed aside, there, where it meets the boulder.'

Peter rubbed his tanned nose. It wasn't easy to concentrate with the cries of both animals hammering at his mind. 'Uncle's in town this afternoon on business, and Aunt Dora's visiting a friend,' he thought aloud.

Fiona gasped. 'But if the poor thing's trapped down

there – '

'Then we have to go after it,' Seb said evenly.

'But we can't! There could be horrid snakes curled up at the bottom – or big rats or . . .'

Seb frowned. 'Shut up, Fiona.'

Peter said, 'She's right but for the wrong reason. The ewe weighs too much for us, and we couldn't get it up.'

'What can we do?'

Barney began to bark and wriggle, not understanding why the other complaining sheep was still hidden from his sight.

Peter had his mind fully on the job at hand. 'I want to go down and see what's happened to the ewe so I'll go back to the farm for rope. I'll dial 999 for the Fire Brigade and be back as quick as I can.'

'The Fire Brigade?' questioned Fiona. 'What can they do?'

'They're trained to rescue animals. Barney, stay.'

Seb shrugged out of his backpack. 'I'll go with you. The rope needs checking before it's used. Fiona, hold on here.'

Fiona dropped to the ground and hugged herself. 'Okay, but hurry. This place gives me the creeps.' She glanced up at the grey cloud that had rolled across the sun. 'Looks like rain.'

Peter and Seb set a brisk pace down the hill, but they still heard Fiona's mournful, 'Barney, stay near, I need company.' And then in a louder voice, 'It's all right, Mrs Sheep, you'll be out soon. I'll look after your baby until then.'

By the time they reached the farm Peter's sense of urgency was at fever pitch. The house remained empty. Aunt Dora and Uncle John had not yet returned. Uncle would know about raising sheep with pulleys and such, but it was anybody's guess when he would be back. Peter dialled emergency services and asked for the Fire

Brigade's help at Viking Farm to rescue a trapped sheep.

In the barn Seb went through the ropes, tossing aside some, keeping others. 'These'll do for a ladder,' he said at last, looping a long one over his shoulder. Peter took the others. 'We'll need a torch.'

Ages seemed to pass before they again reached Fiona on her lonely watch. The trapped sheep still bleated from afar, and Fiona said thankfully, 'Am I glad to see you! I really think we're in for rain.' The lamb backed away on dainty hooves as Fiona came to her feet and gave it a final pat.

The afternoon that had started so full of sunshine had turned grey with heavy ominous cloud, and the first drops of rain hit the dry earth. Peter felt a drop of water on his hot cheek and rubbed it away angrily. More trouble. He tried to put it from his mind as he lifted the fence aside.

Barney watched them curiously. Fiona's face was tight and solemn. 'Will the Fire Brigade be quick?'

'Depends. Fighting a fire comes first, for all Uncle's prize ewe is down there.'

Seb joined two lengths of the rope with professional looking knots. 'This boulder looks solid. We'll tie one end around it, and the other end goes down as a ladder. Peter, tie the torch to your wrist. If you drop it, you've still got it. Just like climbing ropes at school,' he said to Peter as he looped in some knots for handholds.

'Sure thing.' Peter was amazed at the steadiness of his voice when inside he quaked at the job ahead. The hole looked even more menacing in the grey light.

Seb attached a rock to the end of the rope ladder and lowered it until it came to rest at the bottom, marked the length with his hand, and pulled it up again. They looked at the length it had gone.

'Not too far,' Seb said thoughtfully. 'Maybe five metres, about four times your height.'

'I've jumped farther than that!' remarked Peter in an attempt at lightness.

Seb would have none of it. 'Stow it. This is no picnic,' he said with a frown. 'Why does the sheep sound so far away? It can't be right there at the bottom. It must have wandered farther along, down a passage maybe. You'll need a guide so you can find your way back.'

'Like Hansel and Gretel in the forest,' Peter smiled faintly as stout twine was tied to his beltloop.

'You'll be fine so long as you keep your head. Don't wait for a tight spot to say a prayer. Ask for a cool mind *before* you start.' Seb clapped his friend's shoulder and turned away for a last inspection of his work.

Peter bent down to check the laces of his trainers, re-tying them carefully and at the same time talking silently to Jesus. 'Please, help me keep cool and keep me safe.' It seemed to cover everything. They had all done everything that they could think of to prepare for the descent. The rest was up to him.

Chapter Four

Seb said, 'Keep remembering it's just like the climbing ropes at school. Or near enough. With luck you can go down all the way on your own two feet. Like a nice walk, only backward and downhill.'

Peter hated the look of the gaping hole, waiting to take him in and gulp him down like a tasty morsel. Seb sounded confident, but then Seb wasn't going.

Peter hoped that his smile was not as sickly as he felt. 'Right on.'

He took a fresh hold on the rope and backed across the shelf to where the mouth of the hole waited. He reached the edge and looked over his shoulder. The rock surface sloped away into blackness. No bottom in sight. Nothing but rock. Rock, reaching back into the cold, clammy earth. On and on.

Fiona called, 'Good luck.'

Peter's heart thumped so wildly that he feared it would jump from his rib cage, but so far it had not. And it would not, he told himself firmly. His hands gripped the rope so fiercely that he wondered if they would take root.

One foot back, then the other and he was descending. He could not stand upright, the passage was too low, and he had to bend to avoid scraping his head on the rough wall above him. That was a minus. On the plus side the soles of his trainers gripped the surface.

The light was abruptly bad. Drops of rain slanted through the opening above and landed on his cream-white hair. He had left his peaked cap behind, and he wished he hadn't. He could have reversed the peak and worn the familiar gear. He didn't like the feel of rain on his head.

Peter worked his way down the rope farther into the darkness. What was he doing here! He could have waited for the Fire Brigade to arrive. Someone trained for the job could be here now instead of him, feeling his way inch by inch down, ever down to the trapped sheep, but he had to go. He had to know the condition of the animal and offer what help he could. The sheep was his responsibility. He was the shepherd in charge. He risked a glance below and shuddered. Black.

Seb's voice floated to him. 'Try the torch.'

What torch? he thought wildly. Oh yes, the thing tied to his wrist, banging against his arm. Peter wound the rope around his arm, released one hand and grasped the torch. He pointed its beam back and downward, looked over his shoulder and saw more rock slanting away into the dark.

Where was the ground at the bottom? It had to be somewhere below and, having come this far, had to be close! He shifted the torch's beam and found it. 'Gotcha' he muttered grimly. He was panting hard – he seemed to have come miles – and wished that he were back home in the warm, safe kitchen of the farmhouse.

He took a deep breath, covered the short remaining distance quickly and stood erect on firm ground. Nothing but rock around him, and the grey light above was no comfort. He wanted to howl in his sudden isolation. He was alone in this chamber of horrors.

The bleating of the sheep sounded clearer, and his racing heart steadied. Poor thing. Down here for hours. Nothing to eat. No sky above. Once the sheep had started down the slope, it must have picked up speed and been unable to stop until it reached the bottom.

'Hey there, where are you?' he called to it. 'It's okay, I'm on my way. Help's coming. You all right? I mean, anything broken? I know you're not very happy.'

Seb called, 'What did you say?'

'Nothing. I'm talking to the ewe. She's somewhere ahead.' The beam of his torch had found a way to go, an opening in the rock wall.

Fiona's voice reached him. 'If there're snakes, Peter, you come right back up, d'you hear?'

'Fiona, I'm gonna unscrew your head when I get back up! Shut up about snakes!'

Water trickled down beside him. Of course, the rain. It would be pretty heavy up there to be coming down here. He wondered if the hole ever filled with water. In that case, he could float up to the top. But the sheep? Better not to waste time thinking about it and get on with the job.

For good measure he tested his guideline, the twine tied to his beltloop, and started off again, torch in hand.

The air was thick and heavy, once he edged through the opening in the wall. It was a struggle to breathe. Give over, he told himself, it's not stuffy down here. He was finding it hard to breathe because he was terrified.

Forget terrified, he told himself. Forget the passage is narrow. He could see by the light of the torch that there was nothing nasty at his feet. No snakes lying coiled and ready to strike, no fierce rats ready to bite – honestly, Fiona could send him spare some times with her wild talk. There was nothing horrible down here, only a lot of dry grass and stuff blown in by the wind and the bones of some little wild creatures that had fallen in and could not scramble out again.

'How am I doing, Jesus?' he whispered fervently. 'I think I'm doing all right. Not great, but all right, and that's as good as great, isn't it? So long as I'm getting on with the job?'

A few feet ahead and around a bend the ewe came into sight. Peter stared at the expanse of the sheep's rear end. The shearing had been done recently, and the fleece was only beginning to grow again.

'Stuck head first, are you? You look okay from here, the way you're wriggling,' he said in a soothing voice. 'All the same you were lucky to come down without breaking something.'

The bleating was almost deafening in the confined space. Peter propped the torch on the ground behind him and wrapped his arms around the sheep's hind quarters and pulled. The sheep complained bitterly.

'Look, I'm sorry if it makes you cross, but I'm helping you, and this is the only way I know to do it.' He braced himself and pulled again. The sheep popped out from between the narrow rocks like a cork from a bottle and lurched into him. Peter sat down with a thump, his face jammed into the growing fleece.

Peter scooted back on his bottom and stood up. There was no room to turn around. He tugged the heavy sheep back along the short passage and onto the ground where he had first come to rest after his descent.

When Peter returned with the torch, he saw that the trickle of water had turned into a fine spray, and it drenched his head and clothes in the confined space. His shirt stuck coldly to his back.

Peter gulped suddenly. Not only was spray drenching him, but water was spinning down the rocky slope. Puddles of water were forming at his feet, turning the earth and dried grass into a mush, and it wouldn't take long for the place to be awash.

He cupped his hands to his mouth and called, 'The ewe looks okay. Any sign of help?'

'Not yet,' Seb replied. 'Shall I come down?'

'Stay with the rope and keep watching.'

'Fiona's at the lane, ready to open the gate for 'em. How's the water level?'

He swallowed hard. Bits of grass floated around his shoes. 'Okay.'

'Peter, if it gets bad you'll have to come up. Peter, did you hear?'

'I heard.'

The sheep seemed to be searching for a way out. It turned, this way and that way, moving in panic, trying to climb the steep slope and slipping down again. The sheep swerved unexpectedly and slammed into Peter. He staggered back against the hard rock and dropped to his knees, gasping at the sudden pain in his back. The torch hit the rock and went out.

He came to his feet immediately. As much as he wanted to stay still and let the pain pass, he couldn't. He had to be up on his feet to dodge the now wildly cavorting sheep. He clicked uselessly at the switch of the torch. The bump had finished it.

Peter thought of the cleft in the wall and shuffled along, feeling the wall and speaking softly to the frightened sheep, hoping to soothe it by the sound of his voice. The water had crept up to his ankles, and his jeans were sopping from the fall. He clenched his jaw and felt further for the opening, found it and slipped inside the passage. The pain in his back was easing, but he'd have a fine bruise to show for it tomorrow. He could hear the splash of the sheep's hooves as it turned, trying to find a way to freedom.

He began to shake. He could not stay down a minute longer. He was so cold that his teeth chattered. If he waited any longer he would not be able to climb the rope ladder to safety. He gritted his teeth. The rain was warm, his mind told him clearly. Only fear told him otherwise.

No, he must stay. His voice seemed to help the animal

because the frantic splashing had eased. Or perhaps it was tiring? Either way he had to hang in there. Until when? It didn't really matter because he could stay afloat and whatever the level of the water, he could easily swarm up that rope with fear nipping at his heels. But then? Despair at the prize ewe's fate made him clutch his middle. All his effort would be in vain because the ewe would surely drown.

He stopped talking and began to sing softly to the sheep, an aimless 'la la', and so he nearly missed Seb's shout, 'Peter, it's okay. They're here!'

Uncle John drove in as the three excited children reached the farmhouse an hour later, riding squashed together in the front seat of the fire engine between two firemen.

John Styles was a tall, lean man who moved unhurriedly. He had steady grey eyes and the weathered face of a man who spent much time out of doors. He was not given to useless talk and so, when Peter, Seb and Fiona tumbled from the fire engine and ran to him looking exactly like children who had been out in the rain too long, his eyebrows rose to his hairline but he remained silent.

The driver came with them. 'John,' he said by way of greeting, 'Fine now. The ewe came up soft as silk, but I expect you'll want to check for yourself. We left her and the lamb grazing like nothing had ever happened.'

'Harold, what are you talking about?'

Peter spoke up. 'Uncle doesn't know what happened. He was in town all afternoon.'

The driver pulled at Peter's cap. 'Then you'd better tell him. We've got to get on. See you, John.'

'Thanks, Harold, for whatever it was you did.' Uncle John pulled himself together. 'Inside everyone.'

He waited until they were indoors in the warm, fragrant smelling kitchen before he said, 'Let's hear it from the beginning.'

He nearly winced at the barrage of voices that all tried to tell him at once and finally motioned them into silence.

Aunt Dora had returned home some time earlier and had begun preparing the evening meal, but now the simmering saucepans were ignored. Mrs Styles was plump as a farm tabby, fair haired with brown eyes and a head shorter than her husband. She had taken one horrified look at the children when they came in and had struggled ever since to be heard over the clamour. Now she sent her husband a grateful look.

'First things first,' she said. 'Hot baths and dry clothes. Afterwards we'll hear what happened.'

When they came down later, dry and warm, supper was on the table. Peter sat down with one eye on the bowl of mashed potatoes steaming gently before him.

Uncle John gave thanks. 'Dear God, we thank you for this food and for each other. We also ask that these children will speak one at a time to explain just why it was that when I returned from town, I found them soaked, dirty and exhausted and delivered home on the front seat of a fire engine. Amen.'

Everyone echoed 'amen'. Uncle John said mildly as he stood to carve the chicken, 'Peter, perhaps you'll begin.'

Peter said, 'You remember you asked me to check on the flock in the east field? We did.' He helped himself to a mountain of mashed potatoes. 'We found your prize ewe had gone down the hole, the bad one farther up the hill. She'd pushed past the fence to get at the grass.'

Aunt Dora gasped. 'Peter, you never went down there by yourself!'

'I did, but Seb and Fiona were up top. We found some ropes in the barn, and Seb made a ladder. What he doesn't know about ropes, well – '

Uncle John stood stock still with the carving knife

frozen in mid-air. 'By yourself!' he repeated in dismay.

'The ewe's fine and so's her lamb, just like the driver said. I talked to her while we waited down in the hole for the Fire Brigade to rescue her. I think talking helped her, but anyway it sure helped me.'

By the time the meal was over the story had been told by all three participants in the afternoon's event. Aunt Dora had scarcely touched her food. She said at last, 'Peter, you might have been killed.'

Uncle John said, 'Now, Dora, if he'd got into real trouble, the others would have gone for help.' Seb and Fiona nodded in agreement. 'All the same, if it happens again, no more heroics, lad. I can't have my right-hand man in hospital with a broken leg. But the three of you deserve full marks for a job well done. Thank you, all of you. I couldn't have done a better job myself.'

Peter's face turned bright red at the praise. He would remember this evening forever. Wait till he told God in his prayers what Uncle John had said! Uncle was sparing with praise – and criticism, too – so when it came, you knew he really meant it. Uncle was ace. Uncle was the best.

Aunt Dora had found her appetite again and was eating in small, careful bites. She looked up suddenly, her soft eyes bright. 'John, in all the excitement I forgot to ask if you went to the development company this afternoon?'

'I did. I told them Viking Farm wasn't for sale.'

Peter moved in satisfaction and winced. He was sore all over.

– 'And, John, you haven't forgotten that Mike's coming tomorrow? I'll need the car to collect him from the train.'

Peter grinned. With Mike here they would be a proper team again, complete. What was it that the Bible said about a cup filled to the brim? In the psalm that began 'The Lord is my shepherd . . .'? He knew now exactly what it meant. Right now his cup was so full of good things that it was spilling over the brim.

Chapter Five

From his position at the ticket barrier Peter could see the strong, confident figure of Mike Bennett as soon as he stepped from the train. Mike swung along the platform, carrying a blue and yellow bag. He wore new jeans and a matching denim jacket and his dark hair might have started out combed, but it was tousled now. He grinned widely at the sight of Peter, Seb and Fiona waiting for him, and his white teeth shone against his tan.

Fiona hopped up and down in excitement, but then she was only ten, Peter thought, and still inclined to hop when she was excited. Peter considered himself too old for that kind of childish behaviour.

Instead he pummelled his mate's shoulder. 'Hi.'

Seb extended his hands, palms up, and Mike slapped them. 'Hi,' Seb also said.

Mike's grin grew wider.

Aunt Dora kissed his forehead, and everyone was embarrassed by this extreme show of affection. She said, 'Lovely to see you again, Mike. How are your parents? Seb, give him a hand with his bag. Peter, lead the way to the car. Fiona, stay close and don't get separated. So many people in the station this afternoon!'

Peter and Mike's friendship went back a long way. After Peter's mother died and he was left on his own with a stepfather who hated him, Mike had been the friend who had provided protection for his battered mind and body when things were really bad at home.

Seb and Fiona had come into his life only last summer, when they joined with Mike to rescue Peter from the life that had become unbearable. Each of the three had a special place in Peter's affections, but Mike had been there the longest.

Briefing Mike on the events of the past days took them well into the evening, what with time out for dinner and clearing away. The four children sat on the drystone garden wall, chewing long blades of grass. Peter reckoned that they looked rather like Daisy chewing her cud, but he carried on all the same.

The warm light of the long evening lay soft on the valley, thin shadowed by stone walls and the green full-leaved trees. Sheep pulled lazily at the grass, and the last glow of day turned their wool to copper.

When no one could think of another detail to add about the castle that disappeared, Miss Haverly, Leonard or the rescue of the prize sheep, Mike cleared his throat and pronounced judgement. 'Quite a time.'

'You bet.'

'Leonard's still a problem.'

'Yeah.'

'Miss Haverly sounds weird.'

'Right on.'

Peter took the grass blade from his mouth. 'Something else.' The other three looked at him. 'Before dinner I had a call from Miss Haverly. We were having such a good time with Missy's pups, I didn't like to spoil it, but the thing is, she's lost something else. Her favourite milk jug.'

Mike pulled a face. 'How can you lose a milk jug?'

Seb said, 'Maybe the same way she lost all those other things we told you about.'

'At any rate,' Peter went on gloomily, 'she wants us to go over in the morning and find it for her. She said

"Boy, I need sharp eyes again." I wish she'd stop calling me "boy" and remember my name.'

Fiona nodded vigorously. 'She calls me "girl" like I was something under a microscope. I always call her by her proper name, so why can't she do the same for me? I hope you told her we were busy tomorrow, because I don't want to go.'

'I kind of hoped you'd come with me.'

'You never said you'd go!'

'Mmm. She sounded really unhappy. Anyway, why don't you want to help her? You helped me last summer.'

Fiona was exasperated. 'I don't *like* her, that's why. Seb doesn't either, and Mike won't if he meets her.'

All the while Seb had watched and listened to the lively exchange between his indignant cousin and his mildly apologetic friend. Now he spoke up. 'She answered my questions about the castle, and that was nice. She could've told me to shut up. Anyway, Jesus said that we should love our neighbours as ourselves.'

Fiona said darkly, 'Maybe Jesus didn't have a neighbour like Miss Haverly.'

'Come off it! He had neighbours a hundred times worse! Maybe a million times! And some of Jesus' neighbours did bad things to him, but Miss Haverly's only rude. Maybe there's some fruitcake left.'

'That fruitcake was revolting!' Peter exclaimed.

'It was good!' protested Seb.

'Sick-making!'

'Terrific!'

'Knock it off!' Mike levered himself down from the wall and tossed away his chewed grass stem. They all watched him, sensing that the debate had finished and decision time had arrived. He said, 'We'll go with Peter. We don't leave a mate on his own.'

The four children trudged up the track to the awesome gates of Acre Castle next morning. Conversation was sparse. Only Mike's curiosity lightened the heavy atmosphere, but Peter's answers to his questions about what they saw along the way were brief and to the point.

He could have kicked himself for letting them in for the job ahead. They had originally planned a picnic in the hills, beside the little rushing stream that started high in a fold of the hills and tumbled down in a sparkling ribbon of silver. And instead the morning was to be spent inside a dark old castle, looking for a lost milk jug! He must have been nuts to let Miss Haverly talk him into it.

Mike looked up at the rearing, pawing stone lions. 'Sensational!'

They went through the gates, left open by Miss Haverly for their arrival. Mike stopped, planted his fists on his hips and stared at the stone building ahead. 'So this is the disappearing castle! Fantastic! I wouldn't miss this for anything. Lead on.'

Seb came to life. 'It's Norman – '

Fiona groaned. 'Knock it off, Seb. We heard it all.'

Mike said, 'But I haven't, so go on, Seb.'

Seb obliged and by the time they climbed the steps to the heavy wooden door, Mike had been filled in about this leftover from a bygone age.

Miss Haverly patted at her grey hair when she saw them, but it immediately sprang up again at all angles. 'I thought you'd be here earlier. Follow me.'

Peter had been about to introduce Mike, but instead he shot an expressive look at his friend. Mike grinned widely. He was apparently enjoying himself hugely.

Miss Haverly said, 'I remember using it when you were here.' She stopped abruptly, and the line following her knocked up against each other. Peter thought that if she accused them of taking the milk jug, he would march out, but she didn't. She said, 'I put it on the Welsh dresser with the other dishes,' and walked on.

They searched the kitchen from top to bottom. Mike said finally, 'It's not in here. We'll check the other rooms.'

In the living room and dining room he drew back the thick curtains, and new light poured into the rooms. Their hopes sank. Mike looked at the carefully arranged furniture, the neatly placed candlesticks on the mantelpiece, all depressingly tidy. 'No sign of it here, Miss Haverly. We'd better check the downstairs next.'

'Young man, I am not in the habit of putting away my dishes in the cellar!'

Mike said patiently, 'The job's not done until we've looked everywhere. That's why you asked us to come.'

There was no denying the logic of Mike's remark. Miss Haverly led the way down a flight of stone steps built into the thick walls and descending from the entrance hall. At the bottom the cellar sprawled in all directions, dark and shadowy. The low ceiling was a series of arches springing from thick pillars which helped to support the upper storeys. Cobwebs were everywhere.

Mike took one look and said, 'What about the bedrooms?'

Seb put in eagerly. 'We ought to search them.'

Fiona covered a yawn, but Peter bit back a grin. Trust Seb to find a way to satisfy his curiosity about Acre Castle. All the same, he was right.

Mike said, 'Check yours, Miss Haverly, and we'll do the others.'

What did Miss Haverly have against light? Peter asked himself in exasperation when they were on the floor above the living room. He fumbled for a lightswitch inside the door of the bedroom that Fiona had assigned him to check. The light went on and the room sprang into view. It had not been used in years.

Sheets covered the bed and furniture, and the mantelpiece was dusty. Squares of light wallpaper showed that once pictures had hung there. Three pictures. Big ones, too. The lighter patches looked peculiar. Milk Jug? Ha! Not even a forgotten cup and saucer. He switched off the light and returned to the dimly lit landing.

Mike must have found the same because he shook his head at Peter's enquiring look.

Miss Haverly appeared from her bedroom. 'Nothing,' she announced, almost triumphantly, as if they had made a bet and she had won.

Mike nodded. 'And the top floor?'

Seb put in anxiously, 'We'd better look.' He must have had eyes in the back of his head, because he moved aside just as Fiona's sharp elbow aimed for him.

Miss Haverly said, 'You'll find a light at the top of the stairs. I'll wait in the kitchen.'

The steps were built against a massive outer wall and were lit by daylight through arrow slits, which had been glassed to keep out the weather. The steps were stone and so worn that they curved in the middle.

Seb was in awe. 'This is brilliant! Look there on the wall, iron holders for torches!'

'Pooh! I'll take a lightbulb any day,' groaned Fiona. 'Promise me: one look, no more. I don't know where her milk jug is, but this is positively ridiculous! It can't be up here.'

Mike grinned over his shoulder. 'Shouldn't think it is either, but from what I've seen of Miss Haverly, she'd get us back here to check it out. She'd get to wondering and in the end convince herself that this was the very spot it must be, just because we didn't look.'

They emerged from the stairway into a single cavernous room with wooden steps leading up to the battlements. Peter pushed back his cap. 'What about this!'

It was a treasure house. In one corner lay a pile of rusty chainmail, a shield with traces of paint still visible, an iron sword. Nearer to hand was a heavily carved wooden chair with arm rests, the sort on which the knight himself might have sat at official occasions. Old toys, a rocking horse, trunks. Leaning against a wall were paintings in gilt frames. The accumulation of discards from generations of Haverlys.

Seb launched himself into the room, tripped over a coal scuttle and spread his length on the floor. He scarcely noticed. He picked himself and flew to examine the ancient armour. Fiona opened the lid of a leather, brass-bound trunk and drew out a woman's silk patterned dress, long, ruffled, and held it up against her wonderingly.

'Crazy,' muttered Mike and went off to look at a Victorian pennyfarthing bicycle with its enormous front wheel bent out of alignment.

Peter stared. For the first time since arriving he was glad he had come. He could see this was a home where people had lived, generation after generation, secure, solid, making the kind of home that he had and would continue having at Viking Farm. Where nothing would change except the seasons. Where Uncle John and Aunt Dora and he would work the farm, and Anne and Mary would bring their families.

Something had been bothering him, and now it became clear. He said, 'Miss Haverly said no one came up here so why isn't the floor dusty?'

The others looked around. Sure enough there was remarkably little dust on the floor for a part of the house used for storing unwanted items.

Fiona had an answer. 'She probably comes up here a lot and didn't like admitting it. Didn't you see the walls in the bedrooms? Where pictures had been? I reckon Miss Haverly's been selling her things bit by bit – pictures and this stuff – to live on the money.'

Chapter Six

Fiona was strangely subdued on they way home. 'Miss Haverly was almost in tears when we left. I felt sorry for her, but honestly! Getting all worked up over a milk jug!'

The sun was overhead, sending down hot lancing light that made them screw up their eyes against the glare. The castle owner's marmalade cat padded silently from the woods that lined one side of the track, saw them coming and slipped back again into the shadows. A bird called and an unseen forest creature moved in the undergrowth, breaking the noon silence of the wooded height on which Acre Castle stood.

'Maybe it's everything together that's got to her,' Seb mused aloud. 'I mean, she's lost all kinds of things. You know, when something's lost, it means that you expect to find it, sooner or later, but did you notice? While we were searching for her milk jug, we didn't find any of them.'

Peter frowned. Seb was right. They could not possibly have missed a sunhat with a bunch of poppies on it. 'So what're you saying?'

'I think I'm saying that maybe the things were stolen.'

The other three stopped and stared at him.

Mike said reasonably, 'Who'd want to steal stuff like that? A silver-backed hairbrush might be worth a few quid, but a sunhat? The other stuff? They're not worth anything.'

Fiona wiped her forehead with the back of her hand. 'It's the heat, Seb. Your brains are scrambled. Everybody knows Miss Haverly's dotty. She gave the things away, or packed them away, or something like that, and just forgot.'

Peter was not listening. If they hurried, he thought, there was time to take sandwiches up to the stream on the hillside for their lunch. And he knew where it formed a pool and they could splash to their hearts' content. He could almost feel that freezing spring water on his burning skin.

A familiar sound reached Peter, and his stomach knotted in sudden panic. Leonard was out on his motorbike. He would chase them again, like the knight had hunted animals for sport. But the knight had eaten the boar or whatever he took home. Leonard just chased for kicks.

Fiona said uneasily, 'I hear Leonard.'

Mike looked interested. 'The one who chased you?'

Peter nodded. 'There's a short cut up to the castle. We'll wait there until he's gone.'

Seb's chin jutted. 'We ought to face up to him.'

Fiona looked worriedly at Mike. 'What do you think?'

'This is Peter's show.'

Peter said, 'I want to be in the pond in the south field in an hour, and I want to be there in one piece.'

'What're we waiting for? Let's hide!'

They ran across the road, through the bushes and up the path. They were well concealed by the time Leonard cruised by on his powerful motorbike. Peter felt a little silly. The precaution had been unnecessary, because Leonard's bike had been loaded with boxes he was delivering, another of the odd jobs he did. He would have passed them without a glance.

He bounded back down the path, the others close after him. 'Watch out pond, here we come!'

The small parish church was full on Sunday. The age of the Norman church matched the age of the castle, give or take a hundred years. It was small with a square bell tower and thick stone walls. Great round pillars supported the roof and divided the nave, the central section, from each side aisle. There were lovely stained glass windows and an organ.

Peter was on the end of the group from Viking Farm and cut off from a view of the altar by the great pillar in front of him. That was the worst of the old church. If you were unlucky in your seat, you could spend the whole service without seeing a thing. Aunt Dora leaned forward to look along the row of children, and Peter sent her an expressive look.

'Edge up, everybody,' she whispered, and they all squeezed closer together. After that he could see.

The opening hymn had been sung when Peter sensed a latecomer was arriving. And someone who was causing a stir, judging by the murmur of whispering behind him.

Miss Haverly sat down beside him, arranged her worn handbag and white lace gloves on the shelf and opened her service book. Peter felt like groaning. Miss Haverly had not been seen in church since Christmas, and now that she was back, she had to choose him - of all people! - to sit next to. It wasn't fair! She wanted something from him *again* sure as sure, because she was sitting right behind the pillar, and there were other seats with a good view. He'd done his bit for her and wasn't doing any more! He sat stiff and defiant, telling God in his prayers why it was that he wanted nothing more to do with Miss Haverly.

Peter was still determined to stand his ground when Miss Haverly said to him after the service, 'My best china tea pot has gone.'

Peter took a deep breath. 'You should report it to the police, Miss Haverly. My friend thinks your things've been stolen, and I agree.'

'Stolen? Nonsense, impossible. And the police?' Her tone grew sad. 'They'd come and look and be polite to me, but they think I'm, well, a bit strange, just like everyone else does. Don't look so embarrassed, boy, I know what's said behind my back.'

Seated on Peter's other side was Fiona, and she had been listening hard. And now Fiona, who had deeply resented the time and effort demanded by the aging woman, reached across him to take Miss Haverly's thin worn hand in her own strong young one and say, 'Don't worry, we'll come around first thing in the morning.' And it was Fiona who handed her a paper hankie. 'Don't cry, Miss Haverly. Everything'll be fine.'

'Yes, we'll come.' Peter could hardly believe that he was agreeing aloud with Fiona, but he was, and he meant it. When the chips were down, he just couldn't abandon the old woman. It would be cruel, and he hated cruelty.

Strangely, there were no complaints about losing another morning to Miss Haverly. Mike actually looked pleased to be going back to the treasure room, and Seb found a book on English castles and read it between turns at Scrabble that afternoon. Fiona looked kind of smug, which she did when she thought that she had done something especially good. But all she said was, 'Miss Haverly's not so bad as I thought.'

However, next morning all thoughts of Miss Haverly and her latest loss vanished when Uncle John came in to breakfast after his early morning jobs.

He looked bewildered and his face was drawn and grey. He said grimly, 'Thirty sheep were stolen from the east field in the night.'

He sat down and put his head in his hands. Aunt Dora stopped forking bacon rashers onto a plate and stared aghast. 'John, no!'

Peter's face went cold. 'The prize ewe? Her lamb?'

'Both gone.'

Fiona made a little choking sound. Mike came to his feet. He braced his hands on the table and leaned forward. 'Mr Styles, you have to call the police.'

'Sheep rustling?' Uncle John muttered. 'Not a hint of it in the area.'

'Mr Styles,' Mike repeated, 'the police.'

'What was that, Mike? The police? Yes, of course.' He got up heavily, leaned for a moment on the solid wooden table and walked into the hall.

Peter heard the dialling through the thick fog that had entered his mind. They couldn't afford to lose sheep. As for the ewe that had been rescued . . . Who had done this terrible thing to them? His hands balled into fists. He wanted to shout his despair to the four corners of the house, but instead he followed his uncle into the hall and stood close to him until the telephone call was finished.

Uncle John looked down at him. 'They'll be here.' His hand rested on Peter's shoulder.

Peter licked his dry lips and tried to sound confident. 'We'll get the sheep back.' Uncle John pressed his thin shoulder but said nothing.

Aunt Dora hurried in, dabbing her eyes with the edge of her apron. She was close to tears. 'Come and have your breakfast, John. You can't do anything on an empty stomach. Peter, back to the table and finish eating.'

They returned to the kitchen where Fiona sat with her lips pressed tight and Seb looked down at his hands. Mike ate steadily, then took his empty dishes to the counter. Peter looked at his glass of milk but for the world could not bring himself to pick it up. Aunt Dora didn't seem to notice. She put Uncle John's plate in front of him, and he began to eat, but it was clear that he had no idea of what he was doing.

Mike signalled to his friends, and they went outside.

In the open air Fiona's ginger plaits seemed rigid with anger. 'Who'd do such a terrible thing?'

Peter looked off into the distance, then at the house, then at the ground. He didn't seem to be able to focus on anything. 'No idea. Good people live around here, and everybody likes Uncle John.'

'Good people don't steal,' Seb put in gravely.

They all turned to watch a car drive up to the house. The police had arrived.

It was noon before things were back to anything like normal. By then the field had been carefully examined and questions asked and answered. Uncle John had personally phoned around to the other farmers to report the loss, and a meeting was to be held to discuss what might become an outbreak of sheep stealing and how they could best protect their flocks.

Mike said thoughtfully, 'Let's think what we can do to help.' The children sat on the garden wall and watched the police car drive away.

There was a long silence while each put his mind to work. At last Fiona said, 'In the Bible flocks of sheep always have shepherds to guard them. We could be shepherds, too.'

Peter said doubtfully, 'There's a lot of sheep in a lot of fields. We couldn't watch 'em all.'

'But we could watch some. Anything would help.'

Seb asked, 'You mean camp out at night?' He brightened visibly. 'Say, that sounds brill!'

Mike looked up from inspecting the toes of his trainers. 'Good thinking, Fiona. We'll do it. Let's talk to Mr Styles right now.'

Uncle John, however, was not as enthusiastic as the four children. 'Camp on your own?'

'There are four of us, Uncle. We'll be safe enough,' Peter pleaded. 'And anyway, kids all over the world still look after flocks, on their own, some of 'em. If they can do it, so can we.'

Mike spoke. 'We want to help, Mr Styles. We hate what happened last night.'

The idea was tossed back and forth, but surprisingly it was Aunt Dora, who had come in to listen, who tipped the scales. 'Let them, John. If they camp by the stream in the south field, we can see them from the house. They can use that old tent stored in the barn.'

Mr and Mrs Styles exchanged silent messages. Finally he said, 'Very well, but if by chance you do see some rustlers, lie low and report back to me. No heroics. You're my responsibility, and I can't have anything happen to you.'

Seb shouted 'Right on!' and for the first time since breakfast they all laughed.

Aunt Dora disappeared into the kitchen to prepare lunch. The others followed Mr Styles outside to finish the morning's tasks around the farm. Not until the afternoon could they begin to consider the gear they would need to camp.

Seb had inspected the tent and pronounced it serviceable, discouraged Fiona from taking her scrapbook, and was advising on food and clothing when Peter gave a loud groan.

'I forgot Miss Haverly! She's expecting us.'

They looked at each other uncertainly. Fiona sat back on her heels and said unhappily, 'We said we'd go, but it'll take hours and hours. We'll never finish packing!'

Mike glanced at his watch then at the list Fiona was making. 'Seb, you and Fiona carry on here. Peter and I'll go up to the castle and look around. We'll be back as soon as we can. I think we know by now that we won't find what she's lost.'

Chapter Seven

There were visitors at Acre Castle. An expensive new car stood near the flight of steps to the front door, one that Peter could not remember seeing before around the village. The heavy timber door stood open to the warm afternoon, and he knocked to draw Miss Haverly's attention.

At the same time from inside a man's voice reached him, a loud and exasperated voice. 'I don't understand you, Aunt Elvira! I'm offering you a deal that will make us both money, plenty of it, more than enough to see you in comfort for the rest of your life. All you need do is sell this stone monstrosity to me, or rather to my firm, and everything can go ahead. It isn't as if I'm asking anything out of the ordinary. It'll be mine one day, anyway.'

Miss Haverly's voice was thin and high but resolute. 'I'm sorry, Arnold, but I do not wish to sell Acre Castle. It is my home. It has been the home of the Haverlys for generations. I confess I hoped it would someday be your home, too.'

Peter frowned. He could have sworn that Miss Haverly had no family, yet here was a nephew, badgering her from what he could hear.

Mike said, 'Better use the knocker. So much noise in there she won't have heard us.'

'Live *here*?' replied the nephew named Arnold. 'In

this damp mouldy pile of stones? Certainly not! As for you, Aunt Elvira, you'll be much more comfortable in a modern flat. You're not getting any younger. You tell me that you're forgetting where you put things. Now I don't want to alarm you, but you must realise that losing things is a sign, and you need another environment where you can get help.'

'Say it, Arnold. You mean a sheltered flat where I can ring for the Warden when I can't find my teapot.' She sounded more than a little disgusted.

Peter shook himself. It was time to make his presence known instead of eavesdropping. He raised the iron door knocker and let it fall with a resounding crash.

The nephew said, 'Sit still, Aunt Elvira, I'll see who it is.'

A tall, heavy-set man in a dark business suit came from the living room into the hall. He had a thick head of greying hair, a smooth shaven face, and a pink complexion. He looked well fed and, at the moment, annoyed.

'Yes?' he enquired ungraciously.

Peter said, 'We've come to see Miss Haverly. She's expecting us.'

'Who is it, Arnold?' came her voice from inside the castle.

'Two boys. They say you're expecting them.'

Miss Haverly hurried into the hall, and her sudden smile revealed the unnerving sight of the missing tooth. A long fringed shawl trailed from her shoulder, and her bony feet were bare. She looked awful, Peter thought. No wonder her nephew was worried about her.

'Boys, this is my nephew, Arnold Turner.' Peter started to shake hands, but Arnold Turner walked away. Clearly he found their visit unwelcome.

Peter said, 'Miss Haverly, you asked us – '

She shook her head in warning. 'Yes, I asked you to

come by about my cat. Well, it's all right, he's found his way home again.' Peter and Mike looked at each other in confusion. 'Run along, boys, and thank you for offering to find him, but it's not necessary now. Goodbye.'

She closed the door on them.

Peter said, 'What d'you think of that?'

Mike ran his hand through his dark hair. 'She didn't want her nephew to know we'd come to look for the teapot, that's what I think. I didn't like the look of him. I wonder what he's up to?'

They were nearing the gates and Peter stopped to look back at the fine car. 'It has to do with selling up.'

'And she won't do it. He's pushing, but she's not budging. I've got an idea, and it fits everything that's been happening to her. Try this for size. Nephew's trying to get hold of the castle, but she won't sell. Miss Haverly loses lots of her pet belongings. He suggests that she's going dotty because she's losing things. Well, what if we're right and her things have been stolen? Who do you think might be behind it?'

Peter whistled softly. 'Arnold Turner! He wants her to think she's really going dotty.'

'What better way to get her to sell up than to convince her she ought to move to where she can get help?'

The idea turned over in Peter's mind. If Miss Haverly's things had been stolen, that meant someone had to be doing the stealing, and Arnold Turner had a very good reason, indeed.

'Problem is, I can't see her nephew sneaking in and whipping those things, can you?'

'Not really,' said Mike. 'But he could still be behind it. He could have found someone else to take the stuff. I wonder why he wants the castle? What's he going to do with it?'

'An awful lot of stuff is being nicked these days,' Peter

said sadly.

'Rough about your uncle's sheep.'

'I feel sick every time I think about it.'

Peter was so wrapped up in the farm's loss that he came upon Leonard's motorcycle in the lane before he realised it.

He put out a hand to Mike. 'Easy,' he whispered, pointing to the powerful machine parked in the undergrowth.

Mike's eyes widened in appreciation. 'It's fantastic!' He went nearer and touched the shining chrome.

Peter caught a movement in the trees. It was Leonard, coming down the zigzag path that was a short cut to the castle.

Leonard saw them and broke into a run. 'Hey, you kids, get away from that bike!'

Peter's heart pounded. Leonard looked like thunder, and he covered ground like a cheetah after his dinner.

Peter grabbed Mike's arm. 'Let's get out of here!'

They ran for Viking Farm in a blur of arms and legs. Behind them the motorbike burst into noisy life, but Peter didn't waste time looking back. The sound grew deafening. Leonard was on the move, and if they didn't find a burst of speed, they'd be for it!

'Into the trees, Mike.'

They darted off the lane and into the trees. Mike panted, 'If he's really after us, he'll get off his bike and chase us on foot.'

'So what d'we do?'

'Over the wall, twit.'

Peter skidded to a stop, put a foot high on the rough surface of the drystone wall, grasped the top with both hands and launched himself over the top. He landed on his hands and knees in the middle of fresh sheep droppings.

'Yuck!' he shrieked, getting up and staring in horror

at his fouled hands and knees.

Mike landed cat-neat nearby. 'Forget it! Keep running.'

They took off again, sprinting across the field toward the farmhouse, startling the sheep so that they loped away to leave a clear passage. They were half way across when Mike looked back.

'It's okay, he's not coming. He's driving away.' They stopped to listen to the sound of the departing bike, and Peter scrubbed his hands on the grass.

Mike wrinkled his nose. 'You pong something terrible, mate. Two steps behind me, right?'

And so they arrived at Viking Farm.

When Peter had cleaned up and returned to the others in the barn, he found that Mike was reporting the visit to Acre Castle and his thoughts on Arnold Turner and the stolen goods.

Fiona and Seb were listening spellbound, but at Peter's entrance she sniffed the air delicately, decided that it was safe and returned to listening.

Mike finished and Fiona jumped to her feet. 'It makes sense, it really does, and if it's true, it's against everything I ever learned about Jesus' teachings. We have to do something to stop Arnold Turner. Imagine a nephew being terrible to his aunt! Jesus said we're to love our neighbours as we love ourselves, and it goes without saying that we should love our relations.'

Seb shifted uneasily. 'Don't forget the part about loving our enemies, too. Jesus said there's no credit in only loving the people who love you, because that's easy to do.'

'Miss Haverly loves her nephew, and he's her enemy. We'll have to leave it with her.'

Mike help up his hand. 'Hold on! We don't know for sure about any of this. First thing we need to do is – '

'Is to learn more about Arnold Turner,' said Seb

easily. 'Fiona can find that out from Miss Haverly.'

Fiona got up from the floor and brushed her dusty jeans with her dusty hands. Nothing much improved, but she seemed satisfied. 'Leave it to me,' she pronounced confidently.

An hour later she was back, looking so smug that Peter longed to pour a bucket of cold water over her. She said, 'Her nephew owns a development company, and he wants the castle and land for a tourist complex. I figure she started losing things the first time she said she wouldn't sell. I'm sure we're right and Arnold Turner's having his aunt's things stolen.'

Peter suddenly went cold all over. He asked quietly, 'What's the name of the development company?'

'I wrote it down so I wouldn't forget it.' She handed him a slip of paper.

Peter read the name and swallowed hard. 'It's the same one that wanted Uncle's land. Come to think of it, the land around Viking Farm and Acre Castle join up at one point.' He was finding it hard to speak.

Seb took off his glasses and rubbed them against his shirt. 'The combined land would make one big tourist complex.'

'But Uncle won't sell,' Peter finished in a rush of relief.

'Miss Haverly might sell, if her things keep going missing,' said Fiona. 'She's really worried that she ought to leave Acre Castle. What if we told her what we think?'

Mike shook his head. 'Are you nuts? You can't go around accusing people without proof.'

'So we're sure Turner's behind the thefts and why he's doing it, but we can't prove it. What do we do next?'

They instinctively turned to Seb. He said crossly, 'I don't know everything.'

'Be a miracle if you did,' said Mike. 'Okay, we wait

and see what happens next.'

Fiona sighed. 'I was afraid of that. Well, I'm going to my room. Miss Haverly gave me a beautiful Victorian valentine for my scrapbook.'

The boys returned to the work of checking the supplies for the next day.

The camp site was sheltered by a rock overhang and stood beside a small spring where the water welled up from beneath the ground and spilled down the hill until it formed the pool that Peter considered to be his private swimming pool. The sound of the gently flowing stream was as soothing as anything that Peter had heard, not that he needed help going to sleep after the fantastic day they'd had. A long hike in the morning, splashing in and out of the pool in the afternoon, a campfire dinner, and then lots of jokes and talk around the fire.

Through the open tentflap he could see the lights of the farmhouse in the distance where Uncle's meeting about protecting the flocks in the area was at that moment going on. Across the valley and between two of the hills he could just make out the moonlight on the water of one of the many lakes formed by the ice age and the retreating glaciers.

His quiet prayers finished some time ago, Peter settled himself in his sleeping bag and closed his eyes.

On the other side of the tent Fiona wound up her alarm clock. Peter covered his ears against the sound. Only Fiona would have thought to bring a clock! Now the alarm would go off every two hours all through the night, waking them all up when it was time for a change of shepherd.

A crashing of pans brought him bolt upright. Mike's voice came from the dark. 'That's got to be Seb thumping around. Seb, what're you doing in here?'

Seb's voice was apologetic. 'Sorry, I tripped. Fiona,

where's the chocolate?'

'Out!' came three voices at once.

Seb fled.

In the morning Peter returned to the farmhouse to do his work. Uncle had enough on his plate without the added burden of doing Peter's work as well, he had decided.

He yawned after the broken night, but even his turn at sitting beside the campfire and keeping his ears pricked for intruders had been great. He'd watched the stars and moon travel cross the night sky and thought how lucky he was. He had remembered the time in hospital when he first came to live with his aunt and uncle, days when he was treated for the withdrawal symptoms of glue sniffing. They had been bad days, but now they seemed like a dream.

And finally he'd thought about the stolen sheep. 'Dear God,' he'd prayed for the second time that night, 'help us find them.'

Now he swung through the kitchen door and Aunt Dora hugged him as if he'd been gone a month. Uncle John still looked grim, but he managed to smile and ask how things were going.

'We're having a super time. Please, could we stay another night? Please?'

'Any sign of trouble?'

'Not a whisper. Any word about the missing sheep?'

'Nothing. All right then, another night.'

Peter returned to the campsite later, laden with Aunt Dora's good food, and they set off to walk into the hills, Mike leading the way with compass and map.

Peter called, 'I've walked over this land so often that I know it like the back of my hand.' It was an unfortunate remark. Mike and Seb fell on him, pummelling him unmercifully. 'Hey, what did I say!'

'Seb and I are supposed to be explorers! How can we be explorers if you already know everything about what we're exploring!' Mike complained.

'There's that, I suppose,' Peter grinned. 'Forget I said it and lead on.'

They met fell walkers along the way, carrying back packs and following the trails across the rugged hills. The sun was hot and brought out the scents of a hundred growing things. Towards noon they headed back to the camp by another route and when nearly there came upon the scattered remains of an old stone cottage with the stump of a chimney. They stepped over a low stone wall into what had once been a room.

Peter eyed the earthen floor in front of the hearth, puzzled. 'It looks different today.' He crouched down to look more closely. 'The earth's been disturbed, like someone was digging. Odd, really odd.' He scooped away the loose earth and a metal box glinted in the sun. The simple catch opened easily, and the lid fell back.

The metal box was quite full, and on top, covering what was below, lay a broad-brimmed straw sunhat decorated with a large bunch of poppies.

Fiona said in a small voice, 'Guess what's underneath?'

Peter lifted the hat. Miss Haverly's missing things were below it. Seb rubbed his chin in thought. 'Not far from here to Acre Castle. Okay, pack it up and leave it.' He was met with a chorus of disagreement. Miss Haverly's things should be returned at once, the others insisted.

Seb held up his hand to stop the objections. 'If we leave it tonight, we can keep watch. Somebody might add to it, and then we can find out who's the thief.'

Chapter Eight

That night they kept watch in pairs over the buried box of stolen goods. Mike chose the place, an outcrop of rock near the scattering of stone that once had been a cottage.

Peter had the second watch, and Mike was fast asleep beside him. The camp was not far away, but the comforting sight of the fire was lost from view by a curve of the hill. Everything looked different in the night. Nothing looked familiar. Everything was scary. There was deep black nothingness where in daylight there were pleasant grassy hollows and menacing shapes where there should be ordinary rocks and mounds. Peter shivered and pulled his blanket closer around his shoulders. A sheep passed by and his heart nearly leapt from his chest. He hated being here. How did shepherds see the night through alone?

It was too much. He would go spare if he had to endure another moment by himself. He shook Mike's shoulder.

Mike muttered, 'Whassup?'

Mike looked beat. Peter almost wished that he hadn't wakened him. 'How do shepherds see the night through all by themselves?'

'You woke me up to ask me that, you twit!'

'It's lonely and dark.'

Mike yawned. 'Try the Shepherd's Prayer.' He turned

over on the hard ground and went back to sleep.

Why hadn't he thought of that? The very prayer written especially for people in his shoes so very long ago. It was the same one about the brimming cup. Peter put his mind to work. 'The Lord is my shepherd,' it began. Then something, something, and then the part that struck home. He could repeat it word for word, it was so full of meaning right now.

It went, 'Even if I go through the deepest darkness, I will not be afraid, Lord, for you are with me. Your shepherd's rod and staff protect me.' Wow! The old timers knew about fear, too, all right. He felt better now. The shadows again became familiar hollows, and the menacing shapes turned into ordinary landmarks as well known by moonlight as they were by sunlight.

He became aware of someone coming up the hill from the direction of the castle and nudged Mike into wakefulness. This time Mike looked ready to thump him, but Peter put his finger to his lips. 'Someone's coming,' he whispered.

Together they slid down and peered from their cover.

Leonard casually strolled up the hill and into the cottage, crouched down at the chimney stump, scooped away the concealing layer of earth and added something to the buried box. Just as casually he walked away down the hill and was quickly lost from sight.

Peter let out his breath. He felt sick. Leonard was the thief.

He didn't like Leonard, it was true, but all the same he was a familiar figure at the farm, and Uncle John admired his way with the animals.

Mike was on his feet. 'That's that. You okay?'

'I've been better. Crumbs! Who'd have thought . . . Let's get back to camp.'

Together they uncovered the box and carried it back to the camp, built up the fire and woke Fiona and Seb.

'How did Leonard get into the castle to steal?' asked Fiona, covering a huge yawn. 'Miss Haverly wouldn't let him wander in on his own. She locks her door at night, and the windows are too high or too narrow.'

'Only one possible answer,' Seb declared. 'The door that can't be opened because of rust, does open.'

Peter said, 'I've thought it over, and we're not telling Miss Haverly about Leonard.'

'Don't tell me,' Fiona said wearily. 'We're going to help him mend his ways.'

'How did you guess?'

'You've been helping everybody like mad since I got here, Peter James. It wasn't hard to figure out. But why Leonard? He's the pits.'

Mike spoke up. 'Maybe it's because he only took worthless things when he could've taken other stuff that was worth a pile.'

'Got it in one! He stole to order, Arnold Turner's order, I think, because her nephew'd know exactly what she treasured most.'

Seb looked at him shrewdly. 'And you want to help Leonard because your uncle would miss his help.'

'He would,' Peter admitted. He stirred the fire with a stick, feeling awkward, unsure how to put into words the other reason that he had. 'But there's something else. Seeing you all again, well, I keep remembering how you helped me. And now I want to return the favour by giving someone else a hand.'

'You've done enough! Miss Haverly's already had both your hands,' protested Fiona.

'I can't turn my back on this. I wish someone I liked needed help because that's easy, but Jesus said to help anybody. Leonard's the one I'm stuck with.'

'Leonard won't thank you, Peter. He'll just think you're a muggins,' put in Mike.

'Maybe. We'll see.'

Next morning after breakfast Peter left the camp early to do his chores at the farm, and the others packed up. They had not had a sniff of sheep rustlers, but it was good to think that Miss Haverly's thefts were finished. There was no news about the missing sheep.

By noon they found Leonard, working on his bike in his back garden. A leather cord was around his head to keep his long, dark hair back, and the gold stud in his ear showed clearly. He looked up when he heard them coming.

Peter said straight out, 'We watched you last night on the hill. You went straight to the box buried at the old cottage near the castle and put in the collar of Miss Haverly's cat. You've been stealing her things.'

Leonard blinked several times. 'I never went near the place!'

Peter's lips tightened. 'Two of us saw you. We found the box earlier and kept watch.'

Leonard came to his feet and wiped his oily hands on a cloth. He eyed the four children who stared back at him solemnly. 'Push off!' he ordered.

Peter stood his ground. 'We returned the things to Miss Haverly and said we'd stumbled across them, hidden in the rocks up behind the castle.'

'So why don't I see any coppers around?'

'We haven't told them. You're crazy! Risking your neck for a few quid. Now you have to put things right with Miss Haverly. You have to tell her what happened, how you got into the castle, and who hired you. It was her nephew, wasn't it?'

Leonard threw down the cloth angrily. Peter persisted. 'Wasn't it?'

'Hop it, you lot, I've got work to do.'

Mike spoke up, and his voice was cool and even. 'You haven't twigged yet. We don't like stealing from old women, and that's what you did.'

Leonard turned red at the flat description of his wrongdoing, and Peter wondered if Leonard weren't secretly ashamed of himself. Stealing was a lot heavier than chasing kids on a motorcycle, and stealing from a defenceless old woman was the bottom line.

Mike went on. 'It's us or the coppers, believe it.'

Fiona's chin jutted. 'Look, Peter's helping you the best way he knows. He reckons God gave him a hand when he needed it, and he's returning the favour, so to speak.'

'God?' Leonard's chin dropped.

She said tartly, 'You must've heard of God. He made the world, and Jesus is his son. Jesus taught us the best way to live. Heard of him, have you?'

'I heard,' Leonard admitted grudgingly.

'And you still went thieving.' She turned away in disgust.

There was such a long silence that Peter wondered if everything had gone wrong. He had tried his best, but maybe it wasn't good enough? He started to turn, feeling tired and discouraged.

Leonard said abruptly, 'Turner treats me like dirt, he does, and bad mouths his old aunt something chronic. No call for that – she's potty but harmless.'

'Then you'll help?'

Leonard nodded reluctantly. 'It was Turner paid me to nick his old aunt's stuff. I reckon he wanted her stuff nicked to get her to sell the castle. I found out his partners think he's already got the land. If they knew he lied and he didn't have it, he'd be in big trouble.'

Seb spoke up. 'What about the paintings in the castle? The ones that should hang on the walls and don't? Did you steal those?'

Peter looked at his friend in surprise. He assumed that Miss Haverly herself had sold them. Clearly Seb wondered otherwise.

'Don't know nothin' about any pictures.'

Peter saw the honest bewilderment on Leonard's face. 'I believe you. Okay, you have to tell Miss Haverly everything, including the part about her nephew, and there's no time like now. I'll go with you, if you like. It might help,' he added awkwardly, not really wanting to go but knowing that he had to offer.

Leonard eyed him in surprise. 'You'd do that for me?'

'In for a penny, in for a pound.'

The five of them walked up to Acre Castle. The day was overcast and grey, and a hint of fine rain was in the heavy air. Several people watched them curiously as they passed, but Peter didn't notice.

When Miss Haverly opened the door to them he said simply, 'This is Leonard. He has something to tell you.'

An hour later Miss Haverly sat very still in her easy chair holding the marmalade cat in her lap. She had not cried or stormed when she heard that her own nephew had been the cause of her unhappiness. Peter thought that she was brave.

Leonard broke the long silence that followed his confession. 'I'm sorry, Miss Haverly. I wasn't thinking straight. There was this part I wanted for my motorbike and Turner kept on and on at me – He even oiled the rusty hinges on the door so I could get in downstairs. I used the short cut from the lane to get up here so nobody'd notice me,' his voice trailed away miserably.

Miss Haverly straightened. 'You did right to tell me, Leonard. Thank you, everyone, for your help. I shall handle my nephew in my own way.'

Seb spoke up. 'Leonard doesn't know anything about the missing paintings.'

'What missing paintings?'

A small sigh ran around the group. 'You'd better see for yourself. And there's the attic with no dust on the floor . . .'

They went upstairs and pointed out the light patches on the bedroom walls, and then Miss Haverly did burst into tears. 'Oh, Arnold,' she sobbed. 'You didn't need to take them! I'd have given them to you, if you needed the money.'

Fiona took her arm and motioned to the others to leave.

The boys walked silently along the overgrown drive-way to the track, shaken by Miss Haverly's tears. Peter almost wished the paintings had never been mentioned, she had taken it so badly, but the owner would have noticed their absence sooner or later and, reasonably, she would have blamed Leonard. No, it was best that Seb has spoken up when he did.

Aunt Dora came along the lane, carrying a basket of groceries from the village shop. 'Why, Leonard!' she beamed. 'I haven't seen you in ages. Coming back with the boys for lunch?'

Peter nudged him. 'Sure he is. We've had a long morning, and we're starved.'

Leonard shot him a grateful look. 'That'd be nice.'

'And where is Fiona?' Aunt Dora asked.

Seb answered. 'She'll be along soon. She's up at the castle, helping Miss Haverly.'

As it turned out, Fiona telephoned as soon as they reached the house and said that Miss Haverly had asked her to stay to lunch. She said, 'She's still feeling bad, so I'll bake her some of my gingerbread later, and maybe that'll cheer her up. And by the way, there's stuff missing from the attic, too.'

Uncle John walked in as Peter put down the phone, and for a moment Mr Styles's eyes lit up. 'Have the Cheviots been found?'

Peter said regretfully, 'No, that was Fiona. She's stay-ing at the castle for lunch.'

Mr Styles nodded carefully. 'If we don't get them back

we'll have to make do another year with things that badly need replacing.'

'We'll manage, you'll see. What about the beef cattle?' Mr Styles planned to add a small herd to the farm.

'Like always, what we'll get for selling the lambs depends on the market. We could still buy a few cattle if there are no more losses, but it'll be a close thing. You might remember that in your prayers.' He smiled and ruffled Peter's fair hair. 'What's for lunch?' he asked more cheerfully.

'Leonard.'

They both laughed and went into the kitchen.

Aunt Dora was chatting to Leonard as she put lunch on the table. It was hard to tell lunch from dinner at Viking Farm because Aunt Dora believed in plenty of hot cooked meals in a home where everyone worked long and hard. Today there was an enormous pan of toad-in-the-hole with vegetables and home-baked bread, cheese, fruit and trifle topped with cream from Daisy's rich milk. Leonard looked a bit dazed at all the food before him.

He picked up his knife and fork but put them down again when everyone around him bowed their heads in silence. Uncle John said grace, and a flurry of dishes started around the table.

Uncle John said, 'Well, Leonard, dipping starts next week, and I'm counting on your help.'

Aunt Dora said, 'There'll be some lovely Italian clothes this winter, made with our wool.' Mr Styles had sold last month's clip abroad.

Mike and Seb ate quietly. Perhaps they felt awkward with the visitor, after the morning's events. Peter wished he could think of something to say, but for the life of him he couldn't think of a thing.

Uncle John asked, 'And how's the motorbike?'

If conversation had been hard up until now, asking Leonard about his motorcycle opened the floodgates.

Leonard looked up, and his rather sharp features creased with enthusiasm.

'It's great! Last week I was in a race and came in third. Not bad, I think, because all the other riders were older'n me and really experienced.'

Peter's eyes widened at the mass of technical details that followed about size, capacity, make and model of the competitors' machines.

'I tell you, Mr Styles, there's nothing like being on a circuit. The speed, the challenge of holding your own in a field where everybody's good and out to win. Sure it's exciting like nothing else I know, but you've got to concentrate when you're travelling at that speed. One slip and you can have a crash, one second when you're not thinking about what you're doing, and you could sail off the track easy as anything. It's hard, and it takes everything I've got, but some day I'm going to be a champion.'

Everyone was staring as if they had never before seen Leonard.

'Folks around here don't know it, but I've made a pretty good name for myself in the racing world.' He grew embarrassed and tucked into his food.

Uncle John drew a deep breath. 'No, we don't know it,' he said, perhaps thinking of all the complaints about the tearaway who scared the villagers with his bike.

There was a pause while everyone returned to the business of eating. Finally Uncle John said, 'You know we have a youth club at church. I wonder if you'd be willing to come along next week and give a talk about motorcycle racing.'

Leonard looked up in alarm. 'I couldn't!'

'You had us interested, and I'm sure the youngsters would be interested, too. Motorbikes can be dangerous if they're not properly handled, and you can put that message over. How about it?'

'If you're sure – I mean, well. Okay, Mr Styles, I'll be there.'

'Thanks. You could be doing them a favour, starting them off on the right foot, making them think.'

Who would have thought it? Peter mused to himself. Maybe Leonard wasn't such a ratfink after all? And if Uncle John could have a quiet word in Leonard's ear about how he scared the kids with his bike tricks, maybe he'd ease up on the aggro. Peter finished his meal in high spirits.

Chapter Nine

The group from Viking Farm went to the 'home trailing' the following day. Home trailing was a race in which fox hounds ran a ten mile course, following a scent laid down in advance. It was like a fox hunt without the fox, and Peter enjoyed it.

Peter was of two minds about the foxes in the area. They were a danger to sheep, killing young lambs, sometimes full grown ones that were sickly. When it happened, and it did, as he had seen for himself during the lambing season, he hated it. But all the same there was nothing quite like seeing the fine reddish coat moving through the feathery bracken in the misty early morning when the world was not yet awake.

That afternoon everybody who lived in the valley seemed to be in the big field on the other side of the village, dressed warmly against the cool day and the chilly wind that blew from a lowering sky.

Even the rarely seen Miss Haverly was there. Fiona had convinced her to come and had collected her from the castle and walked with her to the field. Peter had to admit that it had been a good idea. Miss Haverly was talking freely to everyone for a change, smiling and nodding, instead of keeping to herself at the castle. No one laughed at her poppy decorated sunhat which she wore with a sheepskin coat.

Leonard had come with his father in an old banger,

and now he off-loaded a fox hound that he called a 'hound dog'. 'This hound dog won't win,' he said confidentially when the boys stopped to watch. 'A good racer in his time, but too old now. That's the winner over there.' He nodded toward a sleek, excited fox hound that strained at its lead held by a local farmer.

'How d'you know it'll win?' asked Seb.

'A little while ago I talked to him, like. Told me he was feeling great today. Don't look so surprised, four eyes. Animals got feelings, too. Not everybody can hear 'em, but I can. I gotta push off now, they're ready to start.'

The noise was ear-shattering. The hounds had caught the scent and were howling, yipping and barking to be away. Knots of people who had been talking together broke up and drifted toward the starting line. Latecomers added their cars to the long row and hurried forward.

Mike found them a good place to watch. 'How long does it take the dogs to run ten miles?'

'About half an hour. They're fast.'

Someone gave a signal, the leads were slipped, and the dogs sped away in a flash of tawny brown, baying at the scent, covering the ground with their long legs at a speed that left Peter gasping. Even Barney, at home now, could not have kept up with these sleek speedsters. They were soon across the field and lost from view in the trees. The sound of their baying died away as they followed the scent trail up into the hills.

The conversation around them turned to Viking Farm and the stolen sheep. Mr Styles shook his head to questions of late news. The opinion was that the thieves had got clean away.

Seb said, 'Come on, let's find Leonard. I've got another question for him.'

They eventually found him leaning against the old

banger, hands in pockets, watching the crowd from beneath his eyelids. Beside him on the bonnet of the car was a bowl of food for his dog. All the owners would reward their runners with food when the race finished.

Seb settled his glasses on his nose. 'Leonard, you heard about the raid on the farm?' Leonard nodded casually. 'Do you have any idea who might've done it? We've talked and talked about it and Peter can't think of anybody who's got it in for his uncle. Mr Styles is beginning to think it was a hit and run theft.'

He shook his head, honestly puzzled. 'Haven't heard anything.'

Seb bit his lip and looked down at the ground. 'What about Turner? After all, if he treated his own aunt like he did, why shouldn't he try to ruin Mr Styles by stealing his sheep? Force him to sell the farm to Turner's development company?'

Peter felt the world spin about him. What was Seb saying! Ruin Uncle John? Force him to sell Viking Farm? His hand balled into fists, and he listened hard for Leonard's answer.

'Hey, you're talking mega trouble. Mr Styles isn't some old woman. He knows what's what, and Turner wouldn't tangle with a man like him.'

Mike spoke up. 'But Mr Styles can't tangle with anybody, because he doesn't know who did it.'

Leonard uncrossed his legs and slowly stood upright. 'Listen, it's gonna be a dark night, and if I was rustling sheep – which you understand I'm not, because how can you steal the sheep you've helped be born? – I'd choose a night like this to do it. The dark's a cover when you cut out a bunch and drive them to the road for loading.'

Seb's mouth was a tight line. 'Thanks, Leonard. Come on, you two, I hear the dogs coming back.'

As they walked away Mike said, 'He could be right about tonight. He's street-wise, or maybe country-wise, seeing as how he lives in the country.'

Peter felt so numb that he found it hard to put one foot in front of the other. A deliberate plan to take away his home? What could he possibly do to stop it?

Fiona and Miss Haverly stood side by side, watching the flow of dogs break over the crest of the hill and spread down the slope, skimming the grassy surface of the field as if they were floating. Fiona had evidently chosen her own particular favourite because she jumped up and down screaming its name, and Miss Haverly covered her ears for protection against the shrieks. Peter watched the finish of the trail race with part of his mind on what had been said.

Leonard's favourite, the dog which had 'told' him he felt great, came in first, and when the last of the field of dogs came in and were feeding, Peter turned to Seb. 'Okay, so how will they steal the next bunch?'

Seb didn't argue the toss about whether there would be another attempt. Clearly he agreed with Peter that it would happen. 'Seems to me it doesn't matter which sheep are stolen. The thing that's the same about stealing any of them is that they have to be taken to a road and loaded on a lorry.'

Mike added, 'What we have to do is keep watch on the lane tonight.'

'Catch 'em in the act,' Peter said fiercely. 'We'll show 'em Viking Farm's not for sale.'

Mike thumped his shoulder. 'Ease up. What could we do if we saw the whole thing? Step up and capture them? I can just hear us: "Okay, you lot, put down those sheep and come out with your hands up! No tricks, we've got you covered with our slingshots." They'd just laugh. No, we need help on this. It's too important, and we have to tell your uncle.'

Seb said, 'We can't talk to him now, the next race's starting.'

It was not until they were home again that they could speak privately to Mr Styles and tell him of Leonard's suggestion that a dark night was a good time for rustling.

But when they proposed that the reason behind the thefts was Arnold Turner's need to get Viking Farm, Mr Styles stopped them. 'No good speculating on the who and the why. First catch your thief, then ask questions.'

Mike whipped out his ever-present ordnance survey map, spread it out on the floor and jabbed the area with his forefinger. 'Few roads, and the only one near the farm is the lane out front. If we keep watch on the lane, we'll see anybody loading sheep from the fields. They have to use a lorry, and the only way a lorry can come is along the lane. What d'you think, Mr Styles?'

'I think you're right. As for the three of you keeping watch – '

The door opened and Fiona marched in. Her mouth was set, and her cheeks pink. 'I heard you out there, don't think I didn't, and I'm miffed! I knew something was going on in here, and am I glad I listened outside the door! That's rotten, really rotten, leaving me out of everything.'

Peter bit back a grin. She faced the boys belligerently, but the effect was spoiled by the fact that she had flour all over her face from her baking and she wore an apron that reached down to her ankles.

'No one's trying to keep you out, Fiona,' Mr Styles said. 'I was about to tell the boys that I appreciate their information, but I can't allow them to help keep watch tonight.'

The four children started talking at once, but Mike silenced the others with a look. 'You'll ask the police to set up a watch?'

'I will. Leonard's idea – ' Mr Styles stopped a moment.

Peter thought it was because he had remembered

Leonard's part in their story. Leonard's thefts had come out in their attempt to convince him that Turner was behind the sheep rustling and the ruin of Viking Farm. Uncle had taken it hard because he liked Leonard. Miss Haverly was not going to report Leonard to the authorities, but he would still have to earn back Uncle John's respect. That would be a stern punishment in itself.

Mr Styles went on. 'Leonard's idea of using a dark night for rustling is a logical one.'

Mike said reasonably, 'Then the more eyes watching, the better.'

This was considered at length. Finally Mr Styles said, 'I won't risk it.'

Peter felt the gaze of his three friends, waiting for him to change his uncle's mind, but Peter knew it was hopeless to try. Uncle never spoke without first thinking, and his mind was made up.

Peter nodded his disappointment. 'I see.' He started toward the door.

His uncle called after him, 'It's for your own safety.'

At this Peter spun around, his face tight with emotion. 'Safety? I'd risk anything to catch them, anything at all,' he said passionately. 'This is my home. You, Aunt Dora, Anne and Mary are my family. I'll do anything to keep us here, run a hundred miles or keep watch all night from behind a bush. I know I'm not smart like Seb, or brave like Mike – or even as quick as Fiona – but my eyes are good, and I know how to keep still. If I saw the lorry or the rustlers or anything else out of the ordinary, I'd go and tell somebody so they could catch 'em.'

Fiona stared at him in astonishment, and Seb nodded wisely.

Mike cleared his throat and unfolded his map again. 'It seems to me this spot right here,' he pointed to the map with his forefinger, 'is the natural place for the police stakeout. They'd have a pretty good view where your fields meet the lane.'

Fiona bent down to look. 'The lane really twists around in that direction! We need plenty of people to keep watch.'

'Not really. If Mr Styles kept watch here – ' He pointed to the spot where the driveway from the farmhouse met the lane, ' – then Seb, Peter, Fiona and I could be in the bushes, somewhere after this curve, there on the other side of the police. The police won't be able to see that far, so it's a natural for us.' His forefinger moved to pinpoint a place some distance from the farmhouse.

Mr Styles looked down at the map, his forehead wrinkled in thought. The children waited, hardly daring to breathe.

At last he said, 'Well, Peter, since you feel so strongly, let's have a good look at what Mike proposes. But as for the rest of you – no, no protests – the rest of you are out of it. And, Peter, no more comparing yourself with others. You suit me just the way you are.'

Peter's grin was as wide as his face as he went to stand by his uncle.

It was dark early that night. No long sunlit summer's evening filled with soft light and long shadows, as it should have been at this time of the year, but a gradual inching from an overcast, grey day into a dark, moonless sky with the stars hidden behind the thick low clouds. Somewhere beyond the valley, up high in the hills it would be raining, but at Viking Farm it remained dry.

Peter zipped up his anorak and at Aunt Dora's insistence checked his pockets for gloves. It might be cold out there, she said, while he sat in the foliage that lined the curve of the lane. The spot at which he would keep watch was a little beyond the place that Mike had recommended and would offer greater concealment. Mr Styles had checked it out as soon as he had finished phoning the police.

Peter was apprehensive now that the time had come to leave the house and take up his position. He'd had a few hours sleep, but he still felt leaden and heavy eyed. Mike and Seb were fast asleep in the bedroom, and he had got up quietly so as not to disturb them. Now he wished he had made some noise and they had awakened and wished him luck.

He would miss them like anything, but it was one thing for him, Peter, to take part in this important stake-out and another for his friends to risk their skins. All the same . . .

'You're sure you'll be warm enough?' Aunt Dora asked. She took the zipper of his anorak up another imaginary notch and smoothed back his hair.

'I'm boiling.'

She handed him the wicker basket. 'Fiona made you sandwiches and a thermos of cocoa and who knows what else. There's enough in there to feed an army. Perhaps you should take an umbrella in case of rain? I don't want you to catch a cold. You remember your last cold – the one that settled on your chest? Well, I think – '

'Aunt Dora, no! I'll be fine, honest! I've got a hood.' Imagine! Sitting under an umbrella on a stakeout! Aunt Dora did fuss sometimes. He checked his watch. Nearly midnight. Time for the baddies to be on the prowl.

Uncle John came in. 'There are two constables on watch at the curve, opposite a field gate. Now remember what you're to do if you see anything suspicious: just slip away and find one of us. We'll do the rest.'

'Got it.'

'Good lad.' He checked his own pockets and took a thermos and a torch from Mrs Styles. 'Well, we've done everything we can to prepare. Let's just hope they come tonight, and we can put a finish to all this. Ready, Peter?'

Peter took a deep breath and straightened his shoulders. 'Ready.'

Chapter Ten

Peter took a bacon sandwich from a plastic box, leaned back against the tree trunk and chewed pleasurably. He had been in position now for half an hour, and already he was hungry. Behind his position was the dry stone wall of a field, and inside the field was the small flock of fine Suffolk rams which fathered the lambs on the farm. The rams were hornless with black faces and stockings, and they were Uncle's pride.

There was no gate here. The gate to the field was farther up the road, opposite the two policemen who kept watch. If the thieves came tonight, and Peter fervently prayed that they would, he hoped they would chose this particular field. Then the rams would be herded through the gate and straight into the arms of the law. Great!

An occasional car drove by, headlights piercing the darkness, and at first Peter shot erect at the sound of each vehicle, but now he watched them pass with a critical eye and didn't move. He was not afraid, he realised with a surge of satisfaction. Not like that night at the ruined cottage with Mike when he had imagined all kinds of strange things.

He could not see the house from here. Earlier there had been a light in the castle shining high through the trees, but now it was gone, and the castle had again disappeared. It was very dark and lonely, but he was managing his fear. Maybe he was too keyed up, too resolved to help put an end to the trouble to let fear get in his way. Or maybe his own precautions were working. When he first settled down, he'd had a little chat with Jesus, asking for courage and clear thinking.

But there was no denying that he missed his mates.

Both Mike and Seb had taken it well, being left out. Fiona had fussed, but not for long, and she had gone to work almost at once, making his sandwiches. She must have worked hours because there were hundreds. Well, lots anyway.

He took another one and froze with it midway to his mouth. Was there a sound? A twig snapping underfoot? Were the thieves out there, approaching on foot? A part of his mind said that sheep rustlers did not walk to the scene of their crime; another part said that he didn't think like a thief, so how could he know?

There! Another sound of brush breaking underfoot. He edged around the tree trunk and peered into the darkness in the direction from which it had come. Instinctively he prepared himself to move quietly through the trees to alert the police watchers.

'Peter?' came a soft call. 'Where are you?'

He knew that voice as well as he knew his own. A huge grin creased his face. 'Over here,' he answered, equally as quiet.

Mike slid down the trunk beside him. 'Hi.'

A few more crunching footsteps and Seb sat down on his other side and wiped his forehead with the back of his hand. 'Meant to be here earlier, but your aunt caught Fiona slipping out and made her go back to bed. We had to wait till things quietened down again before we could get out.'

'You're not supposed to be here,' Peter said, but his tone was light and happy.

'Can't leave a mate on his own.' Mike handed a sandwich to Seb and took one for himself. 'Fiona'll be a problem tomorrow, missing out on this. Maybe we should save her sandwiches for her.'

'You mean she *knew* you were coming? And that's why she packed enough food for an army?'

'Got it in one.' Mike's teeth shone white in the dark. 'All I did was wink, and she knew what we were going to do. Pity she had to make a noise and disturb your aunt or she'd be here, too.'

'Uncle's going to lecture you tomorrow,' Peter warned.

'Face that when the time comes. How about some cocoa?'

For a while it was almost like a picnic, a quiet one and in the middle of the night, but a fine outing all the same. When they had eaten enough, they chose lots to decide the order in which they would keep watch.

By Peter's turn it was all quiet. Mike had drifted off to sleep and Seb's head had sagged sideways until it came to rest against his friend's shoulder. Hardly any traffic passed now, and keeping his gaze on the empty lane made him yawn. His eyelids began to flutter and against all odds he drifted off into a light sleep.

Some time later a sound brought him wide awake and immediately his gaze flew to the lane. Nothing there, but the sound was nearer, a smooth, well-tuned engine approaching in the night. He strained to see. No lights yet, but there should be because the sound was close. He left his place by the tree and crept forward to peer along the lane that curled away into the hills.

A bulky vehicle, no headlamps or sidelights but darker than the night, drove onto the verge and into the undergrowth among the trees. The engine died.

Peter swallowed hard. This wasn't supposed to happen! The lorry was supposed to park near a field gate and load the sheep. The lorry wasn't supposed to park a long way from a gate, next to his own watching place!

On the other hand maybe the lorry was perfectly innocent, the driver stopping for a sleep? Peter didn't believe it for an instant.

He felt hot and cold, both at once. He slid back into the undergrowth and crept to the tree. As quietly as he could, he woke Mike. 'They're here,' he whispered into Mike's ear. 'They're not supposed to be here, but they are. They parked over there, a long way from the gate.' He jabbed the night in the general direction of the parked lorry.

Mike eased upright and woke Seb. Seb rubbed his eyes, but when he started to yawn, Mike clapped his hand over his mouth. He whispered, 'Seb, a lorry's parked away to our left, no lights, suspicious as anything.'

Peter motioned to them to follow and started toward the parked lorry. He had to see what was happening. He had to know what was going on.

And something was going on, he discovered as soon as he worked his way through the undergrowth and came upon the parked lorry, which loomed as a dark patch against the lighter night. The tailgate was being lowered on oiled hinges. It would make a ramp, of course, for the sheep to climb inside.

Mike breathed into his ear, 'They still have to get the sheep out of the field, and the gate's opposite the law. It'll be okay.'

Peter listened hard, and his stomach heaved in sudden despair. 'Negative. They're taking down stones from the wall. They don't need the gate. They're making their own!'

Once identified, the thud of stones dropping on the earth was clear. With no mortar to hold them in place, it was only a question of time until enough stones had been removed from the wall to make an opening.

Mike pulled Seb close and murmured, 'Take off, find the fuzz, they're closest to us, and tell 'em. And careful how you go!'

'What'll you two do?' Seb breathed softly.

'Keep an eye on this lot.'

Seb came to his feet and fixed his glasses firmly on his short nose. One moment he stood beside Peter, and in the next moment he was gone, a faint crunch marking his way through the undergrowth.

Peter said, 'We need to get closer. How many are there, d'you think?'

'Two, maybe three.'

The two boys inched forward until they were within a few metres of the cab. It was empty, and both doors were open. It made sense. The men would avoid the unnecessary noise of closing and opening the doors.

Peter's mouth was a straight, grim line. He could not stay where he was and let this go on. He had to do something, anything to stop it. He eased forward, his mind churning.

Mike's hand grabbed his arm. 'Someone's coming.'

They dropped flat on the earth and lay still. A man in dark clothes approached, leaned into the cab for something and went away again. He passed so close that Peter could make out his black canvas shoes.

The thud of dropping stones stopped, and the complaining bleat of the disturbed rams began. They were being herded toward the opening in the wall. Peter's hands clenched into fists. If only he were as big as Samson from the Bible, the man who toppled the temple by pushing down the pillars! He could have those thieves gift-wrapped for the police in no time! But he was a kid, eleven years old and skinny to boot. He had nothing but his wits. And God's help.

Come to think of it, that should be quite enough!

He began to think clearly. Seb had gone for help. He was completely dependable – Peter frowned suddenly. But what if Seb fell over his own feet? What if he didn't make it to the others? What if right now he was crouching in a ditch and nursing a broken ankle? It was time for Plan B, but what was Plan B?

He leaned close to Mike. 'I'll open the bonnet and whip the distributor cap.'

'A great idea but too tricky. Noisy.'

'Okay, how about this? I'll get the keys from the ignition or let down a tyre.'

'Better, but we'll need a diversion. Look, the first sheep are being loaded. Two men on the job. Give me a few minutes while I circle around. Brainless sheep ought to be easy to spook. Once they're on the move, you check the ignition, and if the keys are there, take 'em. If they're not, get to work on a tyre.'

'If things get sticky, run.'

'That goes for you, too. We can meet up later.'

This was more like it. Simple, straight-forward. They were in with a chance.

Mike slid away into the undergrowth with scarcely a sound, though by now noise was no problem. The sharp clatter of hooves on stone as the rams passed through the opening in the wall would cover any accidental scuffle that Mike made.

Peter started counting slowly to keep track of the passing time. One, two, three – the cab doors were open and all he had to do was wriggle up to the lorry – ten, eleven – slither up into the cab and feel for the keys – eighteen, nineteen – Likely as not they'd be in the ignition because why should the men bother to take them out? However, he should be looking for something to use on the tyre valve, just in case. He kept up the count while he felt around him for a sliver of stone, found a suitable one and slipped it into his pocket.

Presently he caught the swish of a bush moving behind the ramp. Mike had reached his spot and was moving the foliage just enough to cause it to shift unnaturally in the still air. The sheep waiting to be loaded caught the sound and the movement and moved uneasily, sidling and backing. They were spooking all right, Peter thought in satisfaction.

A man's voice muttered with annoyance. Peter wriggled forward on his stomach, saw a sheep break and be brought back to the others. Another bush began to sway and rustle in the quiet air. This was too much for the unhappy flock. The boldest ram broke again, headed away from the unnatural bush toward the open space of the lane. This time it was followed by two others.

The man in charge cursed. 'After them, Jake,' he said. 'They're trying to scatter.' The man called Jake left the ramp and started after the strays. The other sheep milled about, undecided what to do, bleating in confusion.

So there were two men loading, and that must mean there was a third in the field, rounding them up.

By now Peter was at the cab. He lifted his head and checked around him. Jake was out of sight, crashing through the undergrowth that lined the lane, hot foot after the strays. The remaining man worked faster, man-handling some of the flock onto the ramp and into the lorry. And all the time a trickle of sheep passed through the opening in the wall.

Peter pulled himself up into the cab and felt along the dashboard. His fingers trembled so much that when they brushed against the ring of keys he could not fasten on them. He drew a deep breath, clasped them firmly and eased them from the ignition. The lorry would not go anywhere until a way had been found to start it. He had bought time for Seb.

He slithered back down from the cab, reached the ground and wriggled back into the safety of the deep shadows. He unclenched his hand, considered the keys and, with a quick motion, tossed them far into the bushes.

The diversion continued. Mike had no way of knowing

that the job was done. Peter rose to his knees and then his feet, parted the foliage beside him and circled around to join him. Mike stopped moving the bush when Peter arrived, and the two boys prepared to slide away into the night.

At that moment Jake returned with the strays. He passed the bush that until moments ago had been moving and was now absolutely still. He stopped suddenly and muttered, 'What's goin' on here? There hasn't been a breeze all night. Leaves don't move unless there's a breeze.'

Peter felt his face go cold. Their luck had run out, and Jake had finally become suspicious of the rustling undergrowth. Jake took a torch from his pocket, turned it on the bush and found Peter and Mike backing away, shielding their eyes from the abrupt dazzling light.

Jake's face fell in surprise. Peter and Mike whirled around and started running. Jake pulled himself together in a hurry. 'Hey, you two! Come back here!' he shouted.

Peter and Mike pounded on, reached the lane and checked to find their bearings. 'Right or left?' panted Mike.

Peter gulped air. 'Right. Back there we ran away from the lorry. We have to go past where the lorry's hidden to reach the police car.'

'Where's Seb got to?'

'Dunno, but we'd better do something quick because I hear Jake.'

They crossed the lane and entered the shadows on the other side. Behind them the powerful beam of the torch cut the undergrowth and found the lane.

Run or hide? thought Peter.

Mike must have been thinking the same because he said urgently, 'That light'll find us. If we run we have a chance of getting to the stake-out before Jake gets to us. Come on!'

They ran through the trees. They made a lot of noise but there was no help for it. Peter's face was covered with sweat and it ran down his cheeks. Low branches whipped at his body and scratched his hands, bushes tore at his jeans, and always lay the danger of falling over an exposed root.

His heart pumped at double time, and his lungs burned. He ran as he could not remember having run before, tearing through the foliage, stumbling and catching himself before he could fall. And still the long probing light kept pace with them from the lane, shadowing them, finding them, losing them again as they sped through the night.

Jake was slowly but surely closing in. His longer legs and his easier way were winning. Any minute now he would leave the lane, plunge into the undergrowth and grab them.

And then? They were so close to saving Viking Farm that nothing must stop them, but Jake was level with them. Any second he would swerve and pounce . . . Peter clenched his jaw, reached deep inside for a final heroic burst of speed and surged ahead, beyond the torch's beam. The pace was killing, but he must – he *would* reach help. He risked a glance over his shoulder. He was winning the race! Viking Farm was safe because he was going to reach the police, and Jake and the others would be nicked! It was time to get onto the smooth surface of the road . . .

Twin shafts of headlamps swept around the curve ahead and lighted the lane. Jake stopped. Peter didn't. He and Mike kept going, but Peter spared a sideways look at the car that was passing, and then he did stop, full in his tracks. and stared.

It was a police car, its strong headlamps pinning Jake to the lane. And in the back seat, grinning triumphantly through the window, sat Seb.

'I was minding where I walked, that's why it took me so long to get back to the police car. I thought to myself: If I'm not careful, I could stumble and break a leg, and then where would my mates be? So I took it easy all the way. Haste makes waste is what my gran always says. Where do you suppose those keys landed? I can't find 'em,' Seb declared. He shone his torch on the ground in front of him, then circled it slowly around him.

It was an hour later, and until a short time ago this area had been thick with people and police and patrol cars. Now it was quiet again, or nearly so. The four children were combing the area where Peter had tossed the keys of the lorry.

Mrs Styles had come to watch and listen and then had returned to the house to prepare a snack for their return. The sheep had been herded back into the field and Mr Styles was re-building the wall. Not very well, he confessed, but then it was a skill about which he knew little. The local craftsman would have to re-do the job.

Fiona shone her torch on Seb's face. 'I never heard Gran say "haste makes waste". It must've been somebody else.'

'Maybe. Move, I want to check where you're standing.'

Fiona had come with Aunt Dora, burning to know what had happened. It had taken all three boys to satisfy her curiosity, and when the last story finished she had sighed and said, 'And I missed it all!'

Peter had said, 'Don't be stupid, Fiona. It was really hairy at the end. You were better off at home.'

It was perfectly true. It had been hairy, but worth every frightening second. The three men had been taken away by the police, and right now they would be making statements about Arnold Turner and his dodgy development company, and about his plan to steal sheep from Viking Farm until Mr Styles could no longer continue and would have to sell out. And to top it off, they had learned that the thirty stolen sheep, prize ewe and her lamb included, were held at a remote abandoned farm. Now everything would be back to normal. Brilliant!

Fiona said, 'I'm sorry for Miss Haverly.'

'Not her fault her nephew's a ratfink,' said Mike.

'At least her castle's safe. I can't find those keys. Peter, are you sure you threw them over here?'

'Positive. I was right there – ' He pointed his torch at a spot near the cab. ' – and I raised my arm and threw them straight to one side.' He re-enacted the motion.

Seb snorted. 'Then we're ten degrees off. Come on, everybody, let's move to the right.'

Mike yawned. 'I can't forget what a job it was to drag that first sheep away from the others. I didn't know how much sheep like to stay together.'

Peter stared. 'You mean it didn't go off on its own?'

'Not the first time. Once it got used to the idea it took off easily enough the second time.' He grinned. 'It weighed a ton.'

Mr Styles returned, dusting his hands. 'The wall should hold for the night. Are you children ready to go?'

Fiona groaned. 'We can't find the keys, and it's all Peter's fault because anybody who throws away keys ought to know they'll have to be found again.'

Mr Styles laughed. 'We'll search again when it's light.' He looked around at the children. 'It's been a good night's work. Thank you all.' His hand clasped Peter's shoulder,

Mike spoke up. 'About sneaking out, Mr Styles, after you told us not to come here. Seb and I – we're sorry we disobeyed you, but the fact is we just couldn't leave Peter on his own. He's our mate, you see. Our friend.'

'And Peter's lucky to have such good friends. Let's go home. Tomorrow's nearly here.'

Peter grinned. 'And I'm starving.'